DAWN AND THE WE LOVE KIDS CLUB

I was gritting my teeth again. This wasn't what I'd had in mind when I came to live in California. I'd had to leave my other family, upset my friends, work hard to adjust to a new school—and for what? To spend six months with *Dad*. Couldn't he at least have waited till I went back to Connecticut? I suppose he *preferred* to spend time with her.

One thing seemed clear. I wasn't wanted here.

But I was wanted somewhere else, by my mum and stepsister and my best friends.

That was when I made my big decision. I was going to move back to Stoneybrook.

DAWN AND THE
WE LOVE KIDS CLUB

Ann M. Martin

Hippo

*The author gratefully acknowledges
Peter Lerangis for his help
in preparing this manuscript.*

Scholastic Children's Books,
Commonwealth House, 1-19 New Oxford Street,
London WC1A 1NU, UK
a division of Scholastic Ltd
London ~ New York ~ Toronto ~ Sydney ~ Auckland

First published in the US by Scholastic Inc., 1994
First published in the UK by Scholastic Ltd, 1996

ISBN 0 590 13535 X

Typeset in Plantin by Contour Typesetters, Southall, London
Printed by Cox & Wyman Ltd, Reading, Berks.

10 9 8 7 6 5 4 3 2 1

1st CHAPTER

"OK, everyone, that's all," said my maths teacher, looking at the wall clock. "See you *mañana*."

It was the end of a long school day. I chatted with friends as I left class, then got some books from my locker. As I walked outside, the mid-winter breeze felt warm and wonderful.

Stop! What's wrong with this picture?

Number One: no obnoxious bell at the end of school.

Number Two: no coat.

Number Three: no cold weather.

Welcome to California!

I, Dawn Schafer, was back in my home state—the land of beaches and surfing and palm trees and year-round tans. Well, that's an exaggeration. It's a stereotyped idea of California. Nevertheless, it was a different life.

Different from Stoneybrook, Connecticut, that is. That's where I live, technically. This trip to California is a sort of extended visit.

Confusing? Not really. I'm a child of divorce. My mum lives in Stoneybrook and my dad lives here in Palo City, California. (Once upon a time we all lived in Palo City. I was born here and so was my younger brother, Jeff.)

The divorce happened when I was in the seventh grade. Mum whisked Jeff and me off to *her* home town, Stoneybrook, mainly because her parents—my Granny and Pop-Pop—still live there.

I liked Stoneybrook right from the start. We moved into a rambling old farmhouse built in 1795, where I found a secret passageway from the barn to my bedroom! I made some great friends at my new school, and I joined a group called the Babysitters Club (I'll tell you about them later).

As for Jeff, well, he was miserable. He was rude and difficult at home, and he even started getting into trouble at school. Eventually Mum and Dad agreed he'd be better off back in California. It was so hard to see him go. Our house seemed so empty.

But not for long. Mum got married again—to the widowed father of my best friend, Mary Anne Spier. It turned out Mum used to go out with him in high school. (Isn't that romantic?) Mary Anne and her dad moved into our house, and suddenly I had a nice, cosy new family. My life couldn't have been better.

Except when I started thinking about Dad and Jeff.

And thinking. And thinking.

And missing them more and more.

Imagine if *your* dad and *your* only brother lived three thousand miles away. Let me tell you, it feels awful. I'd visited them a couple of times, but that just wasn't enough. I felt as if they were in another world, floating away from me. I needed to spend some time out West. A lot of time.

Mary Anne cried when I told her how I was feeling, but she understood. Poor Mum—she took it personally at first. When she phoned Dad about it, they argued. But that didn't stop them from exploring my idea. They had to talk to academic counsellors at Stoneybrook Middle School *and* at Vista, my California school, to make sure I wouldn't screw up my education if I moved. Then, at last, they agreed I could live with Dad for six months or so.

Which is how I became bi-coastal. (I love that word. It sounds so glamorous.)

To be honest, it isn't very glamorous at all, but you know what? Coming out here was definitely the right thing to do. That aching feeling has gone. It's fun to be with Dad, and I no longer miss Jeff (honestly, I want to throttle him sometimes).

"Hey, Dawn!" a voice called from behind me.

I turned. Our school is actually a cluster of small buildings grouped around a courtyard filled with flowering bushes and juniper trees. Walking across the courtyard were two of my best California friends, Sunny Winslow and Maggie Blume. Sunny was holding out an open bag of vegetable crisps.

"Hi!" I called back.

"Want some?" Sunny asked.

"Yes, please!" Yum. Vegetable crisps are the best. They're like potato crisps, except they're made with carrots and parsnips and sweet potatoes and other great stuff.

OK, it's not so bad. I just happen to like natural foods. That's one thing you should know about me. Luckily, most of my friends here share my tastes, too. (Most of my Stoneybrook friends don't. Mary Anne's boyfriend says I go around gathering nuts with the squirrels, but that's typical boy humour, and I ignore it.)

Having best friends on both coasts is

pretty fantastic. Not to mention belonging to two great babysitting clubs.

That's right. I'm a bi-coastal babysitter. Here in Palo City, I belong to the We ♥ Kids Club (pronounced "We Love Kids Club"). Sunny started the club while I was living in Stoneybrook, after I'd told her about the BSC.

Maggie's a member of the club, too, together with one other girl, Jill Henderson. (Jill lives pretty far from school, so she takes a bus home.) All four of us have blonde hair. Actually, my hair is the lightest (it's almost white). I suppose we could call ourselves the BSC, too, for "Blonde Sitters Club."

Or maybe OFEC, for "Organic Food Eaters Club". Sunny, Maggie and I tore into those crisps on our stroll down Palm Boulevard. It was one of those breezy, warm days when you just feel like doing nothing, and slowly. The sun beamed down and the air was full of familiar southern California scents: flowers, salt air and car exhaust fumes. (Oh, well, I suppose no place is perfect.)

"Do you lot want to have a meeting today?" Sunny asked.

Maggie nodded. "We haven't had one for a week."

"I can't make it," I said. "I've got to sit for Stephie. How about tomorrow?"

"Sounds OK to me," Maggie replied.

"I'll phone Jill," Sunny offered.

Pretty casual, isn't it? That's the We ♥ Kids Club—no rules, no regularly scheduled meetings. *Very* different from the BSC. If Kristy Thomas, the BSC founder, had heard that conversation, she would have had a heart attack. She's a real rules freak. The Babysitters Club is run like a business, with strict meeting times, officers and record-keeping.

I have to admit, at first I had trouble getting used to the easy-going W ♥ KC style. Now I find it kind of refreshing.

Anyway, we chatted and munched for about ten more minutes, till we reached Stephie Robertson's house. I said goodbye to my friends and rang the bell.

"Dawn! Dawn! Dawn! Dawn! Dawn! Dawn!" Stephie screamed from inside.

Stephie is an only child and her dad is a widower. Her nanny, Joanna, usually sits for her. But tonight Joanna was leaving early, to celebrate her birthday.

The screen door opened and out Stephie flew. "Come *on*!" she said, pulling me inside. "You have to see Joanna. She looks so beautiful!"

Joanna came in, dressed in a short fringed skirt and a tight-fitting beaded top, her dark hair pulled back in a sleek, elegant style. She did look great, but also a little embarrassed, as we oohed and aahed over her. Joanna and I quickly went over some last-minute details. Before long, a car pulled up to the kerb, with a very handsome man behind the wheel.

As Joanna climbed in and waved goodbye, Stephie said, "That's her boyfriend. He's a hunk."

I couldn't help laughing. "Stephie, where did you learn that word?"

"*Dawn*," she said, rolling her eyes. "I *am* eight years old."

"Oh."

"It *does* mean something good, doesn't it?"

"Uh, well, yes . . . I suppose so."

"Like what?"

I have to say, Stephie's another reason I like being in California. She's the sweetest, brightest girl I've ever sat for. She used to be painfully shy, but as you can see, she's starting to come out of her shell.

Since she was little, Stephie has suffered from asthma. Emotional stress can send her into a scary fit of wheezing. Luckily that seems to be getting better, too.

Halfway through my explanation of "hunk", Stephie lost interest. "Let's bake," she said. "Dad and I got a cake mix for Joanna's birthday. To surprise her when she gets back later. I want it to be huge with *nine* layers!"

Luckily the packet had enough mix for *two* layers (which was plenty). So we spent the rest of the afternoon in the kitchen. Stephie had a great time. Me? I was disgusted. Do you know how much refined sugar goes into a cake? Tons! I mean, humans weren't *made* to consume that much.

Sigh! Try telling that to an eight-year-old. Stephie thought I was out of my mind.

When we'd finished, the house smelled . . . well, *sweet*.

I hope Stephie was able to keep her dad away from the cake. You should have seen his face when he came home. He was practically drooling.

As for me, I couldn't wait to get to my house and make a fruit smoothie in the blender.

My dad's house is about a fifteen-minute walk from Stephie's. It's beautiful—airy, open and shaped like a square-edged U around a garden. Nearly all the rooms have glass skylights. I love coming home to it.

I ran up the front path and through the door. "Hi! I'm home!" I called out.

"No, you're not. You're *Dawn*!"

That was my brother, Jeff. He had decided the week before that he wanted to be a stand-up comedian. I'd heard that joke five times already. I vowed to myself I would never say "I'm home" again.

"Hi, Jeff," I replied, not encouraging him.

But he barged into the living room, determined to continue the act. "Dawn, what do you call a Smurf in maths class?"

I walked around him towards the kitchen. "I give up."

"*A Smurf bored!*" he said triumphantly, cracking up. "Get it? Like a *surfboard!*"

Our housekeeper, Mrs Bruen, was preparing a salad in the kitchen. "Hello, sweetheart," she said softly. "Just be glad he's not doing those knock-knock jokes—"

Too late. "Knock-knock!" Jeff said.

"Who's there?" I asked wearily.

"Kook."

"Kook who?"

Jeff looked at his watch. "Only one o'clock? Hmm, my watch must be wrong... *Get it?* You said *cuckoo*, like a cuckoo clock!"

(Ugh! Brothers! Sometimes I wonder why I ever left Stoneybrook.)

This went on for a while, till Dad got home from work. "Hello, everybody!" he called as he came inside. "*I'm home!*"

He did it on purpose. I know he did. He *wanted* Jeff to give his daft response.

"No, you're not—"

I put my fingers in my ears.

Dad is one of the nicest guys in the world. Too nice sometimes. He thinks Jeff's new joke habit is just terrific. He laughs at the same lines over and over again. (But I love him anyway.)

"How's my Sunshine?" he asked, giving me a kiss. "Ready for my award-winning vegetable *chimichangas* tonight?"

Without waiting for an answer, he bounded away to change. I suppose I would have said yes to the question. Dad *is* a great cook. But I do have mixed feelings about his *chimichangas*. You see, they happen to be the favourite meal of his girlfriend, Carol. When he makes them, it's a sure sign that she's coming over.

Have I mentioned Carol? Maybe not, but I suppose I should.

Now, don't get me wrong. I like her. She's got a lot of good points. She's young and tries to be hip, she's got tons of energy, and she pays lots of attention to Jeff and me.

Her bad points? Well, she's young and tries to be hip, she's got tons of energy, and she pays lots of attention to Jeff and me.

What I mean is, she tends to go overboard. Sometimes she tries so hard to be cool it drives me crazy. I just want to tell her to act like a grown-up.

When Dad got back to the kitchen, we all set to work. Mrs Bruen chopped veggies, Dad seasoned the sauce and made refried beans, I made a salad dressing, and Jeff cooked the rice.

Sure enough, at six o'clock on the dot, Carol's voice called from the front door, "*Chimi*chang*as*! Mmmm, that smells bodacious!"

Bodacious? Now you see what I mean.

"Hi, honey!" Dad said. "We need your expert taste buds."

Carol bustled into the kitchen. "Oh, you know I've got good taste. I met you, right?"

She giggled. Dad laughed. They kissed.

Me? I managed to hold on to my appetite. But it wasn't easy.

Between Jeff's jokes, Dad's encouragement of him, and Carol's constant giggling, I didn't say very much at dinner. Which was just as well. The meal was fantastic.

But afterwards I felt a little down. I suppose I'd been hoping for a nice, quiet dinner.

I knew one thing that would cheer me up. "Dad, can I phone Mary Anne?" I asked.

"If it's not too late," he said.

I looked at the clock: 7:03. That meant 10:03 at night in Connecticut. I raced into Dad's bedroom and tapped out my Stoneybrook number.

11

"Hello?"

I was in luck. Mary Anne was up. "Hi!" I said. "It's Dawn! Are you asleep?"

"No, I'm reading," Mary Anne replied. "How are you?"

"Fine. What are you reading?"

Mary Anne laughed. "Is that why you rang?"

"No. I suppose I just wanted to, you know, *talk*."

"OK. Well, it's the coolest book. It's called *Julie of the Wolves*."

Mary Anne went on about this book, which is the story of a girl lost in the wilderness of Alaska. I'd read it already, but I listened anyway. It was great to hear her voice. She's the kindest, most sensitive, and most wonderful person in the world.

I don't know exactly why, but I was missing her—and my Stoneybrook family —more than ever that day. And the phone call was only making it worse.

2nd CHAPTER

"Bend your *knees*, Jill. Like this." Sunny got on to her surfboard and demonstrated proper body balance.

No, we weren't at the beach. We weren't even outdoors. Sunny was giving a surfing lesson on the carpet of her own bedroom.

The We ♥ Kids Club had finally got round to holding a meeting. It was Tuesday, five days after I'd sat for Stephie. I'd arrived right on time, at 4:30. Jill was next at 4:36, Maggie at 4:40.

No one complained. (If this happened at a BSC meeting, Kristy would be furious.)

"Go ahead, try again," Sunny insisted.

"This is ridiculous," Jill mumbled. She stepped on the board, which began to wobble left and right. So she flapped her arms wildly and gave us her version of the theme song from *Hawaii Five-O*.

We howled. "Perfect!" Sunny exclaimed.

Sunny's my oldest friend in the whole world. Well, she's not *old*. She's thirteen and in eighth grade, like me. What I mean is, I've known her the longest. We've got lots in common. First of all, we're both outgoing, fun-loving and independent. Second, we've both got blonde hair, although Sunny's hair is strawberry-blonde and mine is almost white. Third, we share the same name, sort of (by pure coincidence, "Sunshine" happens to be my dad's nickname for me). Fourth, we like surfing. And fifth, we adore ghost stories.

The Winslows live down the road from us. Their house is like my second (I mean, *third*) home. You should meet Mrs Winslow. She's a potter who makes the most beautiful stoneware—and she's one of the warmest people I've ever met.

Sunny's full name is Sunshine Daydream Winslow. Yes, I'm serious. (Mr and Mrs Winslow were hippies. Their friends in Oregon, the Johnstons, have two sons called Vernal Equinox and Lunar Eclipse!)

Jill Henderson is actually quiet and serious when she's not carpet-surfing. Of all of us blondes, she's got the darkest hair, and deep, chocolatey-brown eyes. She's the only one who doesn't live in the neighbourhood. Her house is tucked away in the hills on the edge of town. Her parents are divorced, so she lives with her mum and her older sister, Liz. They've got three dogs—all boxers—called Spike, Shakespeare and Smee. (Jill loves them, but those dogs are so ugly!)

I suppose Maggie has the most glitzy life of us all. Her dad's in the film business. I'm not exactly sure what he does, but it must be important. You wouldn't believe their house! It's enormous, with a screening room, a gym and a landscaped pool that looks as if someone lifted it from a tropical island and plopped it in their garden. But do you know what? Maggie hates talking about celebrities and film gossip. Keanu Reeves has actually had dinner at her house, but she didn't tell us till weeks later. To her, it just wasn't a big deal. (Sunny, on the other hand, insisted on touching the fork and plate he'd used.)

Maggie has the coolest look (which is constantly changing). Her hair is short and punkish, with a thin tail at the back. She usually streaks it purple or green or black. Her fashion sense runs towards leather bomber jackets and lace-up black boots.

What happens at a W ♥ KC meeting (besides surfing)? Well, we talk, snack and answer some phone calls for babysitting. Neighbourhood parents can count on us whenever they need an experienced and reliable sitter.

Great idea, isn't it? Little do any of the local parents realize that they have Kristy Thomas to thank.

That's right. As far as I know, no one had ever dreamed up a babysitters club before Kristy did. She's amazing that way. Ideas burst out of her all the time.

She invented the BSC to help her mum, who was a single parent trying to bring up four kids. Since then Mrs Thomas has remarried, this time to a really rich guy called Watson Brewer, who had two kids from a previous marriage. Now the family lives in a mansion—with an adopted little sister, a grandmother, and several pets.

Kristy's got brown hair and brown eyes, is great at sport and always dresses casually. Although she's the shortest BSC member, she's got the strongest personality. In case you haven't guessed, she's the club chairman.

Every BSC member has a title and certain duties. The club meets from 5:30 to 6:00 on Mondays, Wednesdays and Fridays. Parents know they must phone only during those times. The club advertises around town and has *tons* of clients. How do they keep track of all of them? With another Kristy invention: the club record book, which has a client list and a calendar of our appointments. Club members also have to write about each sitting experience in the club *notebook*. (Yup, Kristy's idea, too.)

If the BSC were a car, Kristy would be the starter—but Mary Anne would be the engine. As club secretary, she keeps things running (she's in charge of the record book). Kristy and Mary Anne are best friends. They even look alike, although Mary Anne's brown hair is cut really short these days. Personality-wise, they couldn't be more different. Mary Anne is quiet and super-sensitive. It doesn't take much to make her cry. Her boyfriend, Logan Bruno (the one who calls me "Runs With Squirrels") carries a box of tissues when they go to the cinema together. Needless to say, she's the world's best, most caring sister. Before our parents married, she never had a brother or sister or a mother. Her mum died when she was a baby, and Mr Spier brought her up by himself—*very* strictly, too. (Fortunately, being married to my mum has loosened him up.)

Claudia Kishi is the club vice-chairman, mainly because her room is BSC headquarters. She's Japanese-American and absolutely *stunning* (thin, too, despite the fact that she's a junk-food fanatic). Claudia is the most talented person I know—in drawing, painting, sculpting, jewellery-making, even fashion. She can create the coolest outfits out of odd combinations of clothes. Her spelling is creative, too—and her maths. In other words, Claud isn't a great student. Her parents used to wish she could be more like her older sister, who's a real genius, but I think they've given up comparing.

The BSC's other fashion-plate (and treasurer) is Stacey McGill. She's very sophisticated, but not snobby. She was born and brought up in New York City, and her dad still lives there (she's another "divorced kid"). Her duty is collecting club subs on Mondays and paying our expenses—like Claudia's phone bill. Stacey and I have some important things in common: divorced parents, blonde hair (hers is darker), and healthy eating habits. She has no choice about *her* diet, though, because she's diabetic. That means her body can't control the amount of sugar in her blood. She can't eat sweets, and she injects herself daily with a substance called insulin. (I know, it's awful, but she can't help it.)

Oh. My BSC title was alternate officer. I could take over anyone else's job in case of emergency.

All the BSC members are eighth-graders, except for Jessi Ramsey and Mallory Pike.

They're our junior members, and they're both in sixth grade. They usually take early sitting jobs, as they have to be home at a certain time. (Hating this is one of the many things they have in common.) Talk about talent! Jessi's a gifted ballerina, and Mallory writes and illustrates her own stories. Jessi is the club's only African-American, and she had to deal with a lot of prejudice in Stoneybrook when her family moved in. She's the oldest of three kids. Mallory is the oldest of *eight* kids, so she's kind of a round-the-clock babysitter. Recently Mal's been recovering from glandular fever, so she hasn't been active in the club.

How does the BSC deal with two absent members (Mal and me)? By relying on its two *associate* members. Usually the associates just take the occasional job and are excused from attending meetings. But nowadays one of them, Shannon Kilbourne, has taken over my job as alternate officer. Shannon's the only BSC member who goes to a private school (Stoneybrook Day School). She's involved in all kinds of extracurricular activities there. I don't know how she finds time for everything.

The other associate is Logan Bruno. Yes, Mary Anne's boyfriend. Even though he's a carnivore and sports freak, I like him. He talks in this cute Kentucky accent, and he's great-looking. He's been handling some of the sitting overload, too.

I've been in touch with all the BSC members, but mostly with Mary Anne. They're all flabbergasted that the We ♥ Kids Club has lasted without strict rules.

It is pretty amazing when you think about it. Parents can call any of our numbers whenever they want. Whoever gets the call takes the job, or lines up someone else. Sunny has a record book at her house but we don't use it much, as the calls come in at all our houses. Somehow we always seem to work things out.

Our meetings, as you've already seen, are very casual. (Sometimes we even hold them outside.) Officers? No way. Punctuality? It might as well be a foreign word.

Bleeeep! The phone chirped as Sunny was explaining to Jill about waxing surfboards.

Sunny grabbed the receiver from her bedside table. "We Love Kids Club," she said. "Hi, Mr Robertson . . . Yes, we're all here. . . A week from Saturday? Hang on."

(At this point in a BSC meeting, Claudia would tell the parent she'd call right back. Then she'd hang up while Mary Anne was carefully looking through the record book, checking every possible scheduling conflict and trying to make sure each member was getting a roughly equal amount of work.)

Not the We ♥ Kids Club. "Dawn, are you busy that day?" Sunny asked with her hand over the mouthpiece.

"I don't think so," I replied.

"OK, Mr Robertson, Dawn'll be there," Sunny said into the phone. "'Bye."

End of conversation.

Eventually Sunny put her board away and we turned to our other favourite topic— food. The W ♥ KC has a health-food cookbook, and each of us keeps a file of personal recipes that we update all the time.

Maggie was in the middle of describing a scrumptious noodle dish with sesame paste and watercress, when the phone rang again.

"We Love Kids Club!" Sunny announced into the phone. "What? Who *is* that? Come off it! Is that *Ellen*?"

I smiled. Ellen Bliemer is a friend who loves practical jokes. Once she called as a radio DJ and convinced Sunny she'd win a thousand dollars if she named some obscure rock tune.

Sunny's brow became more and more wrinkled. "Uh-huh . . . OK . . . I suppose so . . . er, can I call you right back?" She rummaged in her bedside table drawer, took out a pencil and a piece of paper, and scribbled a number. "Got it. 'Bye."

We were staring at her as she hung up. "What was that about?" I asked.

Sunny looked dumbfounded. "She says she's a feature-story writer from the *Palo City Post*—Miss Lieb."

"Rhonda Lieb?" Maggie said. "She wrote about my dad once."

"Oh my lord!" Sunny's face was turning red. "Maybe it wasn't Ellen."

"What did she want?" Jill asked.

"She said she's writing a series of articles about kids who run businesses. She heard about the We Love Kids Club and wants to make an appointment to interview us."

"*What?*" I squeaked.

"Hey, let's do it!" Jill said.

"When?" Sunny asked.

"How about tomorrow?" I suggested.

Maggie nodded. "OK with me."

"Me too," Jill added.

"Try the number she left," I said. "If the newspaper answers, you know she's genuine."

Sunny smiled weakly. "You do it. I feel like a total dork for asking if she was Ellen."

Me? Call the biggest local newspaper to arrange an article about the W ♥ KC? No need to ask twice!

Looking at Sunny's scribble, I tapped out the number.

A voice barked, "Positydeskenfeet, murbletch!" (Well, that was what it *sounded* like.)

"Uh, hello? Is that, er, Miss Lieb?"

"*Rhonda! Line t—*"

Silence. I was on hold.

A moment later a much nicer voice said, "Hello, Rhonda Lieb speaking."

"Hi, my name's Dawn Schafer, calling about the We Love Kids Club—"

"Oh, yes, thank you for getting back to me so soon. You . . . sound different."

"Well, the girl you talked to is . . . indisposed right now." (I'd heard that word on TV. I hoped I'd used it properly.) "But our club has decided that tomorrow would be all right for the interview."

"Great! About this time? Say, four-thirty?"

"Four-thirty?" I echoed.

Sunny, Maggie and Jill nodded so fast I felt the draught.

"OK," I said. Then I gave her Sunny's address.

"Terrific. See you then."

"'Bye."

The moment I hung up, the room practically exploded.

"We're going to be famous!" Sunny shrieked.

"Where did she hear about us?" Jill asked.

"Is she bringing a photographer?" Maggie wanted to know.

We were higher than three kites. If the phone had rung for a sitting job, I'm sure we wouldn't have heard it. Mrs Winslow knocked on our door to make sure a bat hadn't flown into the room or something.

The We ♥ Kids Club in the *Palo City Post*? Now *that* was cool.

3rd CHAPTER

Ding-dong!

It was 4:47 on Wednesday. My friends and I had gathered at Sunny's house. I suppose Miss Lieb was as casual about time as the W♥KC is. She was seventeen minutes late. We'd been sitting on the living room sofa for at least half an hour, waiting.

You know how it is when you're all keyed up for a long time. You get rather jumpy.

"She's here!" Sunny screamed.

We all sprang up at once. Maggie's green hair-tail whipped me across the face. Jill, who was eating a wholewheat cracker with cashew butter, chewed furiously and wiped her hands on her white jeans.

Sunny reached the door first. She pulled it open and Miss Lieb breezed in. "Hi! Rhonda Lieb," she said, shaking Sunny's hand. "Sorry for the delay. You must be Sunny."

Miss Lieb was much younger than I'd expected. She had short brown hair, a friendly smile, and was wearing a beautiful cotton cardigan over a white T-shirt and grey leggings. She could have been a college student.

We introduced ourselves nervously. (Well, *Maggie* wasn't nervous. She's had dinner with Keanu Reeves.)

Mrs Winslow must have heard the commotion, because she came into the room and offered Miss Lieb some coffee.

Moments later we were sitting around the living room. Miss Lieb opened her shoulder bag and pulled out a cassette recorder. "Does anyone mind if I tape you?" she asked.

"No," we said.

"Fabulous. Let's get started. The purpose of this series of articles is to spotlight the youthful spirit of enterprise in this area—show the community the *good* things that are happening with our kids. I'm talking to a youth-run car wash, a kids' video company, and a tutoring cooperative. I heard about your group through the principal at the Vista School." She looked at us for a response.

We all kind of grunted postively. Sunny

was sitting at the edge of the sofa, looking as if she would fall forward. Jill's legs were crossed tightly to hide the cashew butter stain. Maggie was fiddling with a pencil.

Mrs Winslow laughed as she came into the room with a cup of coffee. "What's happened? Is she giving you a maths test?"

That did it. We giggled, and the tension began to lift.

"You know, I used to babysit, right through college," Miss Lieb said with a smile. "I was studying to be an actress, and one day I took an eight-year-old charge, Rena, to an ice-cream shop. In walks this famous director who starts talking to *me*."

"Wow!" I said. "Did he give you a part in a film?"

"No, but he gave Rena one. That was when I decided to become a journalist."

We groaned in sympathy. I liked Miss Lieb already. She seemed like one of us, only grown-up. Soon she began asking us questions. She especially wanted to know about my bi-coastalism, Maggie's Hollywood lifestyle, and our interest in health foods.

We explained how the group was organized (which didn't take long). Then we talked about our experiences. Sunny told her about a charge who insisted on taking a carrot to bed every night. Maggie mentioned a girl who poured bubble bath in the dishwasher. Jill described a baking experience with twins, which ended up as a pastry fight. I gave her a cooking story too, about a neighbour I'd sat for who liked mixing toothpaste with milk and cereal for his dinner.

By the time I'd finished that last story, we were roaring with laughter. Even Miss Lieb was practically falling off the sofa.

At about five-thirty a photographer arrived. He introduced himself as Lance and he was, well, a hunk. He was in his twenties, dressed in black, with dark brown hair pulled back in a ponytail, and the deepest, most luscious eyes I'd ever seen.

"I'd like to catch you all in a variety of shots," he said. "Some casual, some posed."

"OK!" we cried. I think Lance could have asked us to weed the lawn and we'd have agreed.

We went outside. Clover and Daffodil, the two little girls who live in the neighbourhood, were playing with their friends Sara and Ruby. Miss Lieb soon managed to persuade them to pretend they were charges (actually, they all are, every now and then). We posed individually and as a group. We went to Sunny's room and pretended to have a meeting. All the while, Lance kept snapping away. He must have used five rolls of film.

When we finally emerged from the house, a crowd had gathered in front. (I suppose Clover and Daffodil had spread the word around.)

The crowd parted to let Miss Lieb and Lance get back to their cars. It was like the Oscars. One kid even held out an autograph book to them, although I'm sure he had no idea who they were.

As for us, well, I noticed most of the goodbyes were being directed at Lance.

The article didn't appear for five days. Five long, agonizing days.

Each morning the newspaper arrived with a plop on the front doormat. Each morning I carefully checked the features section. I looked at every headline, every little blurb. I even checked the other sections, in case the article had been misplaced.

But there was no mistaking it that Monday. The headline at the top of the features page looked like this:

Palo City ♥s the We ♥ Kids Club:
The Story of a Babysitting Business
by Rhonda Lieb

Under the headline was a photo of the four of us. Sunny had just hit a beach ball in the air, and was laughing. Maggie and Jill were running after the ball with one of the neighbourhood kids. And I was watching nearby.

Near the end of the piece, we appeared again, smiling in a posed group close-up that was labelled with each of our names.

Have you ever seen your name and photo in print, knowing they're going to be seen by thousands of people? It's breathtaking. I actually shivered.

I was never a speed reader, but I must have zipped through the article in about three seconds. Here's how it began:

> Who says you can't have fun while you're working hard? Must have been someone who never met the We ♥ Kids Club.
>
> That's right. We ♥ Kids. The name says it all. It was a love for children that brought Sunny Winslow, Maggie Blume, Jill Henderson and Dawn Schafer together. And they've become the hottest babysitting foursome around. (Come to think of it, what parent could resist hiring caregivers with a group name like theirs?)

The article continued from there, describing us and the club. I was "a silken-haired beauty with a laugh like pealing bells" (hey, *she* wrote it, not me). Sunny was "an aptly named fireball of boundless enthusiasm". Maggie was "savvy, hip, and just this side of *au courant*" (whatever that means), and Jill was "warm and nurturing, the calming force of the group".

I couldn't believe she was talking about us!

I ran into the kitchen to show Dad and Jeff. Dad's face lit up when he saw the article. "*Hey!* My daughter the celebrity!"

"Looks like there's a spider on your face in the bottom picture," was Jeff's comment.

"Ha, ha!" I replied. The insult didn't bother me one bit. "Be right back!" I flew through the house and out of the front door.

A short distance from our house is a news-stand. I cycled to it and bought ten copies of the newspaper. Of course I had to show the article to Mr Klein, the shop-keeper—and he cut out a copy of it to put in his window.

Then I raced home and began writing a letter to the BSC. (I would have phoned Mary Anne, but it was 10.30 A.M. in Connecticut and she'd already be at school.) I was halfway through the letter when the phone rang.

I knew it would be one of the W ♥ KC members. "I'll get it!" I shouted, running into the kitchen.

Sure enough, it was Sunny. I could tell by her scream. "Aaargghhh! I can't believe it!"

"I know! It's great!" I said. "You . . . you 'aptly named fireball'!"

"Huh?"

I laughed. "That's what the article called you! Didn't you read it?"

"Oh! I wasn't talking about *that*. Dawn, we're going to be TV stars!"

Now it was my turn to say "Huh?"

"You know Chuck Raymond, the reporter on the local news? He just phoned me!"

"You're kidding!"

"I mean it! I'm sitting here eating breakfast, the phone rings, and I answer it with my mouth full of Shredded Wheat. I say 'Huwwo?' and this voice at the other end says, 'This is Chuck Raymond from WPCN, is Sunny Winslow there?' Well, I nearly choked. I coughed and got this wheat shred stuck up my nose. It was horrible!"

"Oh, my lord, what did he want?"

"He goes, 'Our producer saw the article in the paper this morning and he thinks it would be a good human-interest angle for the evening news programme. I wondered if we could bring a crew to your house, say, on Wednesday?' Something like that."

I screamed. I couldn't help it. Dad, who'd been shaving in the bathroom, came running into the kitchen to see if I'd just had an accident. He stared at me, stupefied.

"Did you say yes?" I managed to ask.

"Yes! But I forgot to ask you lot!"

"That's OK! Oh, Sunny, this is *so* exciting!"

Dad was still in the kitchen when we hung up. He's not the type to go crazy over things like this, but even his jaw dropped when I told him the news.

Jeff? Well, let's put it this way. I didn't hear one joke (or insult) escape his mouth during the rest of the day.

I discovered something on Wednesday. Being a star is boring.

At first it seemed incredibly glamorous. The camera crew was at Sunny's house when the four of us got back from school. Our neighbours had crowded around to watch. Workers with headphones and WPCN T-shirts were keeping people away from the lawn. Scratchy conversations squawked out of walkie-talkies left and right. Wires snaked around, held down with silver tape. The crew looked ready to start shooting at any minute. Or so I thought.

Mrs Winslow was out on the pavement, talking to Clover, Daffodil, Ruby and Sara—as well as some other kids who had dropped by. As we arrived, the kids cheered and swarmed around us.

"Ready for fame and fortune?" Mrs Winslow asked with a big smile.

Behind us, a sharp voice called out, "Are you the girls?"

We turned to see a bearded guy with a baseball cap approaching us.

"Er, yes," Sunny answered.

"Hi, I'm Stu, the A.D.," he said. (That stands for assistant director.) "We're still setting up, so Tina will go inside with you to do make-up and hair, OK?"

A gorgeous red-haired woman appeared behind him, holding a bulging satchel.

"OK," Sunny squeaked.

We marched inside with Mrs Winslow and Tina. Twenty minutes later we emerged, looking like film stars (at least I thought so). The crew was still setting up. The kids were playing on the lawn. Chucks Raymond was nowhere to be seen.

We sat on Sunny's porch and chatted. And sat and chatted.

Then we stopped chatting and just sat. And sat. . .

The crew set up white sheets on square frames. Then they set up lights on tripods.

34

They argued and moved the white sheets. Then they argued and moved the lights. Then they talked into their headphones.

Honestly, I don't know how real film actors do it. I was totally drained of energy after an hour of this.

At last Chuck Raymond turned up with the director, a very tanned, very chic woman called Marisol.

The two of them rounded up the kids and told us to begin playing. "Have some fun!" Marisol said. "Be natural."

Oh, of course! Be natural, with fifty people swarming around, pointing microphones and cameras at you. No problem.

"Playing" never looked so stiff. We W♥KC members were lifeless from the wait, and the kids kept looking into the cameras. One of the boys got hit on the head with a plastic ball and began to cry. Terrific.

Chuck Raymond, bless his heart, knew just what to do. He's a fantastic mimic, and he put on a little act for us. (I could see Jeff in the crowd, looking at him in awe.) Soon we began to relax. Tina rushed over to freshen Mr Raymond's make-up and put *spray paint* on a bald spot on the back of his head (yes, really). He turned to the camera as we played on the lawn, and began his talk: "Here in Palo City, four extraordinary young women have become the most popular people in the neighbourhood. . ."

He sounded natural, but he was actually reading the words from an electric screen next to the camera. After a few "takes" of that, we went into the living room, where he interviewed us. Each time anyone said something, it had to be repeated immediately—once so that the camera person could shoot the speaker, and again to shoot the listener's reaction. (They were going to edit the film to make the interview look like one conversation.)

By the time the crew left, it was pitch-dark outside. All four of our families (including Carol) were now at the Winslows', and we decided to celebrate by going out for an early dinner.

As we made our way to the cars, Sunny said, "Dawn, do you realize how long everyone was here today? This is going to take up the whole news broadcast."

"Maybe it'll be a special report," I replied.

For about the twentieth time that day, we squealed and hugged each other.

"Makes me puke," Jeff said, plopping into the back seat of Dad's car.

The broadcast was scheduled for Friday night. Carol turned up after dinner with a director's chair for me, tied with red ribbon. The word DAWN was on the back, in the middle of a gold star. A pair of sunglasses and a visor hung from the arms.

I wore them as I made a huge bowl of popcorn. Sunny, Mr and Mrs Winslow, Jill and Maggie came over half an hour before the programme, with nuts and muesli bars and crisps.

We gathered around the TV. I checked and double-checked the VCR to make sure I'd programmed the tape properly (which didn't really matter, because everyone I knew was taping it). Jeff tried to act casual, but he was so excited he couldn't sit still.

"Good evening, and welcome to the eight o'clock news," the newsreader said.

My friends and I squirmed and looked at each other. I grabbed Sunny's hand.

Well, we sat through the international news. Then some advertisements. Then the national news. Then more advertisements. The weather. The sport. *More* advertisements. Then. . .

"Now we go over to Chuck Raymond, who has the story of a very unusual business, whose customers are, well, some pretty happy parents. Chuck?"

This was it. Our big moment. Now we were *all* clutching hands. Mrs Winslow was starting to cry.

Chuck Raymond appeared, saying his introductory piece, looking as if he were making up the words. In the background, we were running around and laughing. The way the camera was angled, you couldn't see any wires or white sheets or crew or staring neighbours. It looked as though Chuck Raymond had just happened to pass by Sunny's house with a microphone in his hand.

"There you are!" Carol exclaimed.

Sunny, Jill, Maggie and I were silent, eyes wide and mouths open.

The camera cut to the living room—and me, describing the club! I nearly died. I looked so . . . wide. And pale. But I didn't really care. I was on TV!

They cut me off at the end of a sentence. Then Maggie said a few words, Sunny told about a sitting experience, and Jill nodded enthusiastically. A few more outdoor scenes, and it was over.

"That's it?" Jill said.

Maggie looked at her watch. "Four minutes. That's not bad."

A whole gruelling afternoon for four minutes. How weird.

Ah, showbiz! At least I now had a *lot* more to include in my letter to the members of the BSC.

Not to mention a videotape to send them.

4th CHAPTER

"You look so different!"

Stephie was in awe of my TV performance. She told me she'd fallen asleep during the broadcast, so I brought her the tape when I sat for her on Saturday. She made me play the W ♥ KC segment five times.

"I look like a ghost," I replied.

Stephie shook her head. "Oh, no. You always look so pretty, Dawn."

I do love Stephie. And not only because she says nice things about me.

Our friendship has really grown. When I first met Stephie, she was this frail little thing with terrible asthma, who always seemed on the verge of crying. Whenever I talked to her and tried to draw her out, she'd only nod or give one-word answers.

So I decided not to force anything. I just

quietly made myself available to her. Little by little she began opening up, and I discovered a sensitive, fun-loving girl. The more I got to know her, the more she reminded me of Mary Anne. (In fact, when my friends in the BSC visited Palo City, Stephie and Mary Anne grew pretty close.)

Like Mary Anne's mum, Stephie's mum died when she was a baby. Stephie has talked about her only once, very matter-of-factly. She said that since she couldn't remember her mum, she didn't feel any sadness. (I wondered if she was telling the truth. Mary Anne doesn't remember her mum, either, but she often cries when she thinks of her.)

A month or so after I started sitting for Stephie, her dad told me her asthma was improving. He was convinced it was because she was happier. (Stephie's attacks are usually brought on by emotional stress.) That made me feel good!

Now Stephie and I are almost like sisters. She always asks for me to sit for her when Joanna's out.

Our video clip was fading on the TV. "Thank you, Chuck," the female news-reader said with a bright smile. "It's nice to know local parents can leave their kids in good hands."

"Almost makes this bachelor want to go

out and start a family," the sports announcer said with a chuckle.

"Oh my, Gary, is that a proposal?" the
newsreader asked.

They both started laughing. (Ugh!) I
reached for the remote control.

"Is she *single*?" Stephie asked.

"I suppose so," I said. "But I think those
kinds of jokes are written in advance."

"Oh. Too bad. She's so beautiful. Did
you meet her?"

"No," I said. "Only Chuck Raymond."

"Rats! I wish my dad would date someone like *her*."

Aha, a matchmaker! Yet another side of
shy Stephie Robertson. "Well, if I find out
anything about her, I'll let you know."

"I like your dad's girlfriend. Wouldn't it
be great if they got married? Then you'd
have *two* mums."

"Yes." (To be honest, it didn't sound
great at all. It was something I was trying
hard not to think about.) "Don't worry. I'm
sure your dad will meet someone nice."

She shrugged. "Probably not. He hardly
ever goes out any more."

I switched off the TV. "You really want a
mum, don't you?"

Stephie looked at the floor. "I suppose so.
I used to pretend Joanna was my mum, but
I don't any more. It's not the same." She

suddenly smiled and stood up. "Want to see something?"

"OK."

Stephie ran upstairs to her room. I heard a drawer open and close. When she came back, she was clutching a smudged old envelope. She held it out to me and said, "Open it."

I did. Inside was a typical school photo— a bookcase in the background, Stephie looking into the distance, smiling awkwardly with a tooth missing.

It wasn't a very good picture. Stephie's dress was old-fashioned, her hair looked weird and stiff, and she seemed heavy.

Then I realized something. Stephie didn't have any missing teeth.

And the date scrawled in the margin was almost thirty years ago.

I gasped. "Stephie, is this. . .?"

"My mum," she said. "Doesn't she look like me?"

"Oh, wow! This is incredible!"

Stephie carefully put the photo back in the envelope. "I like to look at it sometimes. I pretend we're talking to each other."

My throat tightened. I could feel tears coming to my eyes.

Stephie ran upstairs to put the photo away. When she came down again, she said she was dying to go outside.

We spent the next hour or so playing catch and riding bikes. Stephie saw a kid do a wheelie, and tried desperately to do one herself.

She couldn't, but I was impressed. She used to hate physical activity.

On our way home, Stephie said to me, "You're fun, Dawn. I wish you'd stay in Palo City for good."

"Oh, Stephie, I wish I could, too. But I'd miss my other family."

"My teacher told us one day people might be able to clone themselves into identical twins. That would be so cool. Then you could be in both places."

"I'll find the laboratory and sign up," I said.

Back at Stephie's house, we ate a big cheese-and-cracker snack. Mr Robertson was due home in fifteen minutes, so I mentioned to Stephie that I would have to leave pretty soon.

"Can we draw?" Stephie asked.

"OK," I said.

Stephie found some blank paper and crayons. "Let's draw our families."

"All right."

I used a pale green crayon to draw a rough map of the United States. On the right side I drew three people: my mum, Mary Anne and Richard (Mary Anne's dad). On the left side I drew Jeff and my dad. I couldn't decide on which side to draw myself, so at last I decided on the top of the map. I drew a blonde girl with hands stretched to both coasts.

Then I looked at the West Coast side and realized I hadn't drawn Carol. I felt guilty. She was *like* family, sort of. I think she and dad are in love, and she's at the house all the time.

Then I thought, *No*. She wasn't related. That had to be the requirement.

I added a surfboard and a bright sun on the West Coast. As I was deciding how to decorate the East Coast, I glanced at Stephie's paper.

With her tongue poking out of the corner of her mouth, she was busily drawing four people next to a house. I looked closer.

A small female and a tall male were obviously her and her dad. Between them was a woman. I decided that was Joanna.

But on top of the paper, floating in the sky over the three figures, was a second woman. "Who's that?" I asked.

"That's my mum," Stephie said. "In heaven."

I looked again. Her mum's face had a huge smile, and wings were coming out of her dress.

Then I looked at the other woman, the

one between Stephie and her dad. She was wearing a white dress with a funny kind of hat that drooped over her face.

"Is that Joanna?" I asked.

"No," Stephie said, shaking her head. "That's what my new mum will look like one day."

I realized what her outfit was.

A wedding dress with a veil.

5th CHAPTER

"Wait! One at a time. What was the last name of the people who phoned you, Jill—Van Druten? How do you spell that?" Sunny was frantically flicking through the W ♥ KC record book. It hadn't been opened for weeks.

Usually, when we *do* use the book, we all just write our own jobs in it. But this time Sunny thought it would be easier if one person handled the scheduling. (This is about as organized as the W ♥ KC gets.)

"V-A-N, space, D-R-U-T-E-N," Jill replied.

"And yours, Maggie?" Sunny said.

"Smith. S-M-I-T-H."

"Duh. Thanks for the help."

Maggie suddenly let out a gasp. "Oh, *no*! I think I've double-booked myself! Is the eighth a Tuesday?"

"Hang on." Sunny closed the address section of the book and turned to the calendar. "No, it's a Monday."

"Phew!" Maggie said.

"What are you talking about?" I asked, looking at the calendar on Sunny's wall. "It *is* a Tuesday."

"Nope," Sunny insisted, holding out her book. "Look, Dawn."

I glanced at it. "Er, that's last year's, Sunny. Look at your wall."

Sunny's eyes widened. "I knew I forgot to get something at the stationery shop."

What a meeting! A week had gone by since the TV broadcast. As you can see, things were becoming a lot less laid-back.

If the history of the W ♥ KC is ever written, I think it'll be divided into two eras: BF and AF. Before Fame and After Fame.

Our phones were ringing day and night. I don't know *how* some of those people found our numbers. Maggie got a call from a parent in San Diego (I suppose because she's the only Blume in our county's phone directory). Maggie had to explain patiently that Palo City was more than two hours away. I got a call from a very young-sounding boy who wanted me to send him my autograph. Sunny was grilled by an eighth-grade girl who wanted to start *her* version of the club in another town. Not to mention all the actual babysitting jobs that came in.

Neither the Palo City Press nor WPCN had publicized our phone numbers (for reasons of privacy) but they got tons of calls asking about us.

Great, huh? Well, yes and no.

I'd always thought of the Babysitters Club as a tight ship, and the We ♥ Kids Club as sort of a surfboard riding the waves. Each was fun in its own way.

Now I realized the W ♥ KC was in danger of wiping out.

Sunny yanked the calendar off the wall. "This will be our official calendar until I get a book-sized one," she said. "OK, let's start again, one by one. Tell me who phoned, and the date and time you're supposed to sit. Dawn?"

I was holding four scraps of paper in my hand, on which I'd written the information. "Let's see, I said I'd sit for Stephie on Thursday . . . two new kids, Sarah and Nathaniel Walden, on Friday week . . . a girl called Catya McMullen next Saturday . . . Erick and Ryan DeWitt on . . . oh, *no*!"

Thursday, I had scribbled. The same day I'd agreed to sit for Stephie.

"I've double-booked, too!" I said. (Me, veteran BSC member, of all people! I imagined Kristy wagging a finger at me.)

"Wait! Wait! Wait!" Sunny said, writing furiously. "What day was Catya—"

Bleeeep!

I picked up the phone. "We Love Kids Club!"

"Hello, my name's Lisa Schwartz, and I saw your article in the paper," a voice said. "We've just moved into town, and we're wondering if you have a brochure."

A brochure? "Er, no, we haven't at the moment," I said, "but one of us will be happy to meet you and your children."

"Well, I need someone this Friday. I'd love it if one of you could come half an hour early and meet my two boys."

"*The Facklers called you?*" I heard Sunny suddenly say to Jill. "They called me, too!"

Mrs Schwartz heard her, too. "Is this a bad time?" she asked.

"No, not at all," I lied. "Let me take your number and call you back in a few minutes."

I wrote the number down, hung up, and plunged back into the roaring surf.

Sunny told me the current problem. Not only had Maggie and I both double-booked sitting jobs, but somehow Mr and Mrs Fackler had double-booked two different *sitters*!

"What a mess!" I said.

Sunny let out a big sigh. "Let's solve one thing at a time. What should we do first?"

"I suppose I could phone Mr Robertson and the DeWitts," I said, "and see if I can sit for the kids together."

"I'll do that, too," Maggie agreed.

"I bet the Facklers will phone one of us when they realize what they did," Jill said to Sunny. "Then the one who gets the call can call the other."

"What if they don't call?" Sunny asked. "And if they do, which one of us should take the job?"

Jill shrugged. "We could both go, and split the money."

OK, that was it. I'd had enough. It was time for us to paddle to shore and build a ship.

Or at least a nice, sturdy raft.

"I hate to say it," I began, "but maybe we should talk about making rules. I know we're different from the Babysitters Club, but things are getting out of hand."

I'd had this conversation once before with Sunny. She had insisted that the W ♥ KC didn't need to be as rigid as the BSC. Up till now, she'd been right. We'd never had as many clients as the BSC did. But that was obviously changing.

I expected everyone to protest. Instead, they just looked at me.

"What shall we do?" Jill asked.

"Well, first of all we should decide on regular meetings," I said. "Then we make some leaflets to hand out and stick up in public places—leaflets that say parents should only call during meeting times, and use Sunny's phone number. This way we can easily record our jobs. That's how the BSC works. We also have officers, so nobody gets confused about who does what."

"I don't like the idea of *officers*," Maggie complained. "Like, 'Aye-aye, Captain Sunny.' That seems so official."

"We don't *have* to do everything exactly the same as the Babysitters Club, Maggie," Jill replied. "Maybe just *some* things."

"Or we can make up our own rules," Sunny suggested. "Stuff that makes sense for us."

Maggie shrugged. "As long as we can be flexible about it. No attendance sheets or penalty points or secret handshakes and stuff."

Sunny's eyes lit up. "Ooh, secret handshakes! I *like* that idea!"

"Me too!" Jill said.

For the next few minutes, we tried out different We ♥ Kids Club handshakes—behind our backs, under our legs, jumping in the air. At last we collapsed from laughter.

By the end of our meeting, we hadn't decided on any changes. But we did agree that *something* had to be done.

For the time being, we'd just try to cope.

And buy a new calendar.

6th CHAPTER

Monday

Hurray! A ☆ is born! And to think, we knew you before you laughed like pealing bells! Will you still remember us at the Oscars?

Seriously, I am so proud of you, Dawn. Claudia got your package Friday, and she called us right away. We had a special meeting at four o'clock. Thanks for sending all those copies of the article. Claudia gave a dramatic reading of it, especially the great description of you. Then we watched the video about ten times.

Janine hooked up a second VCR and made a tape for each of us, so when I got home I watched it some more. Now I know it by heart.

We do have one problem, though. I think Kristy is a little jealous, and her Idea Machine is going wild ...

Did I tell you that Kristy is a complicated person? Well, she is.

Ninety-nine out of a hundred Kristy ideas are fantastic. But there's always that one stinker.

From Stacey's letter, I could tell that Kristy was on her way to another one.

It started at that Friday BSC meeting. Everyone went crazy over the article and the video. Even Claudia's sister, Janine, watched it. (Janine's comment was "very good production values".)

Afterwards the members of the BSC retreated to Claudia's room.

"This is so cool!" Stacey kept saying.

"I think Dawn's telegenic," Shannon said.

"You believe in that stuff?" Claudia asked.

"Huh?" Shannon looked at her blankly.

"Reading minds and everything?"

Shannon threw back her head and laughed. "That's tele*path*ic! Telegenic is like 'photogenic on television'."

Then Kristy spoke up. "*We* should make a video."

"That would be great," Jessi piped up. "We could do a take-off! Daddy does an excellent TV announcer impression—"

"No, I mean *really* make one," Kristy interrupted. "Hey, if the We Love Kids Club could be on TV—"

"Kristy," Stacey said, "you don't just *make* a video and put it on TV. The news station contacted the We Love Kids Club. No one's contacted us."

"Well, why not?" Kristy snapped. "We've been around longer than the We Love Kids Club. If it weren't for us, they wouldn't exist!"

"OK, so they were lucky," Stacey replied. "Maybe one day we'll be lucky, too."

Luckily the phone started ringing with sitting jobs before Kristy could answer Stacey. It was past five-thirty. Kristy was so worked up, she'd forgotten to call the meeting to order. (I think that must be a first in the BSC history.)

I should explain something. As I mentioned before, Kristy and Mary Anne are best friends. They grew up as next-door-neighbours and started playing together when they were still in nappies.

When I moved to Stoneybrook, *whoosh!*

All of a sudden Mary Anne became my best friend, too, and then moved into my house and became my sister. You can imagine how Kristy felt. I wasn't exactly her favourite person. Luckily things settled down in time. Kristy and I became friends and stayed friends. But a little germ of tension never quite went away.

I suppose the germ started to grow again when Kristy saw the article and video. (At least that was Stacey's opinion.) There I was on TV. First I'd "stolen" Kristy's best friend, then taken her greatest idea to a group of girls who got it all wrong, and now *they* (and I) were getting all the glory.

By Friday the germ had become a raging flu.

That night Kristy babysat for her younger brother (David Michael), her stepsiblings (Karen and Andrew), and her adopted sister (Emily). When she'd put them to bed, she read the article and watched the video again.

I can just see the wheels turning in her head. I'm sure she *tried* to put aside her feelings about me. I'm sure she thought she was just cooking up another idea to help the Babysitters Club.

Whatever was on her mind, here's what she decided: if the TV stations and newspapers weren't coming to her, she would go to them.

The next morning, Saturday, she decided to "pitch" a story about the Babysitters Club to the news. ("Pitch" means "try to sell an idea". Kristy had heard that term on TV and liked it, probably because it sounded like baseball.)

She began making phone calls. The first one was to the *Stoneybrook News*.

News switchboard, may I help you?" an operator asked.

"Hello, my name is Kristy Thomas and I'd like to speak to the person in charge of, er, publicity for—"

"Please hold," the operator interrupted. (I *hate* it when that happens.)

Click . . . rriiiing! "Children's calendar, weddings and obituaries," a voice said.

Well, it took a while for Kristy to reach the right department. When she did, the response was, "We're booked up with features for a while. Have you tried your school paper?"

That wasn't the response she wanted—so she tried the Stamford newspaper (Stamford is the nearest city to Stoneybrook.) They were even less interested.

Next Kristy tried the two local television stations. The first one wouldn't let her past the operator.

She tried a different tactic for the Hartford station. She actually wrote a script for her "pitch".

Somehow she got through to a station official. As soon as she heard the woman's voice Kristy barged ahead, trying to read her script in an adult voice: "Hello, this is Kristy Thomas of the Thomas Talent Agency, and I have exclusive rights to the story of an extraordinary organization known by every parent in the Southwestern Connecticut radius. It's called the Babysitters Club."

Kristy took a deep breath. The woman said, "The what?"

"The Babysitters Club."

The woman burst out laughing. "Is this some kind of a joke?"

"No!" Kristy shot back. Then she remembered her mature voice: "I mean, imagine, an answer to the age-old problem of parents everywhere—"

"Have you got a tape?"

"A tape?"

"If you represent this act, or whatever it is, you must have a tape."

Kristy hadn't worked that into her script. "Er, well, I'll have to . . . call you back."

That blew it. Kristy would have to go back to the drawing board.

One thing about Kristy, she never gives

up. She couldn't wait to bring up her big plan at the Monday BSC meeting. She thought everyone would be excited about the idea. Maybe they could make a tape of their own and send it to the station.

As soon as the meeting began, she re-enacted her pitch. The reaction? Total silence.

"So, what do you think?" Kristy said. "Should we make a tape?"

Claudia and Stacey exchanged a Look. So did Shannon and Jessi. And Mary Anne and the floor.

At last Stacey spoke up. "I don't remember deciding we were going to contact the media."

"Of course we did!" Kristy protested. "Remember on Friday when we said we never got on TV or in the papers—"

"Well, yes, but we didn't say anything about actually *trying*," Stacey said.

Kristy shrugged. "What's so terrible about trying?"

"Kristy, you're the one who's always lecturing us about group decisions," Claudia said. "You went and did this without telling us first."

"But—but—" Kristy spluttered, "I didn't think anyone would mind something like this!"

"Remember when Mary Anne got her

hair cut?" Stacey asked. "We felt a little hurt because she hadn't told us in advance that she was going to do that."

"Well, that was stupid of us," Kristy replied. "We all agreed."

"But this isn't," Shannon piped up. "I mean, why do we need *more* publicity, Kristy? Dawn's in California, Mallory's at home recovering from glandular fever and calls are coming in like crazy. We can hardly keep up with the jobs as it is."

"I've just had a phone call from Dawn," Mary Anne said. "It sounds as if the We Love Kids Club is going crazy."

"That's because they're not organized!" Kristy exclaimed. "They're hardly even a club."

"Look," Stacey interrupted. "We said we didn't want to take in new members to replace Dawn and Mal, right? If we get any more publicity, we'll have to recruit half of SMS."

"We could hold our meetings in the gym," Claudia suggested.

"You'd have to order M&M's by the truckload," Stacey said.

"Oh, that reminds me!" Claudia cried. "Get off the bed."

Mary Anne jumped off and Claudia reached under the mattress to pull out a huge bag of peanut brittle. "Food break!"

"I thought the bed felt rather lumpy," Mary Anne remarked.

Jessi laughed. "Mary Anne Spier, the Princess and the Pieces."

Everyone groaned. At last the meeting was getting back to normal. Sort of.

Kristy grabbed a handful of sweets and munched away, but she was glowering. She hardly said a word for the rest of the meeting.

Reading about this incident made me feel a little guilty. Maybe I should never have sent that article and video.

Oh, well. At the end of Stacey's letter, she promised she'd keep me posted on the "Kristy Crisis".

7th
CHAPTER

Thursday was my double-sitting day.

I was lucky. Mr Robertson and Mrs DeWitt were as nice as could be when I explained what had happened. They agreed that I could take Stephie over to the DeWitts' and sit for all three kids there. Erick (who's eight) and Ryan (six) were happy that she was coming over.

Stephie, on the other hand, didn't seem too pleased with the idea.

She hardly said hello when I picked her up. And she was practically silent as we walked to the DeWitts'.

At last I said, "Stephie, are you angry about something?"

"Yes. I *hate* Erick and Ryan."

"But I thought you didn't know them very well."

Stephie looked at me as if I'd said the

stupidest thing in the world. "They go to my school, Dawn. And they're nit-heads."

"What makes you say that?"

"It's just true." She stared at the ground and pouted. "And I know why we're going there. You *forgot* you were sitting for me, so you said you'd sit for *them*. And you said we were like sisters. Sisters don't forget!"

No wonder she was upset. I stopped walking and crouched down next to her. "Oh, Stephie, I just made a mistake. You wouldn't believe how many phone calls I got after the We Love Kids Club was on TV. It was all so confusing, I couldn't think straight. I promise it will never happen again."

"I wish that TV show had never happened," Stephie said under her breath.

"Hey, do you want to know a secret? When I went to your school, sometimes we wrote 'NP' on our palms."

She gave me a baffled look. "Why?"

"It stands for Nit Protection. Just in case. Here, give me your hands."

She did. I took out a pen and wrote a tiny "NP" on each palm. "There," I said, "now you can't catch nits."

A tiny smile appeared on her face. "Are we still like sisters?"

"Of course."

She looked admiringly at her tiny NPs. "Well . . . OK."

Phew! Stephie stayed in a pretty good mood—until we reached the DeWitts' front lawn.

There, duelling with plastic swords, were Peter Pan and Captain Hook.

"Blast you, Pan! I'll cleave you to the biscuit!" Ryan shouted.

"*Brisket*, dummy!" Erick replied.

Ryan lowered his sword. "Uh-uh. No such word."

Erick lunged forward and whacked Ryan's sword away. "You're a codfish, Hook!"

"Hey, that's not fair!" Ryan protested.

At last Erick looked in our direction. "Look! There's Wendy and Tiger Lily."

Stephie was glaring at them. I could tell she had no intention of being Tiger Lily.

Luckily the front door opened just then, and out walked Mrs DeWitt. "Hi, Dawn! And hello, Stephie. Oh, look at you. Just as pretty as always!"

Mrs DeWitt is tall and thin, with huge brown eyes and a wonderful smile. She's an actress and has been in tons of advertisements.

Ryan, who had disappeared behind the house, now came back with a long rope.

"Erick, you tie up Tiger Lily and I'll rescue her."

Stephie looked horrified.

"Ryan Martin DeWitt, you put that rope away!" Mrs DeWitt ordered. She smiled at Stephie and nodded, "They're just excited to see you."

Stephie stayed glued to my side while Mrs DeWitt quickly gave me some instructions. Then she looked at her watch and said, "I have to run. Have a good time. I've left a snack inside for you and the kids."

"Snack time!" Erick shouted. "Yea!"

"First come and say goodbye." Mrs DeWitt knelt down and the boys ran into her arms, almost knocking her over.

"Will you be back in time to tuck us in?" Ryan asked.

"Long before that, sweetheart," she said, kissing his forehead. "And so will Daddy." She wrapped them both in a huge hug. "Be good."

The boys ran inside.

As Mrs DeWitt walked towards her car, Stephie called out, "'Bye!" with a wave of her hand.

"'Bye, dear!" Mrs DeWitt replied. "Have fun."

Stephie beamed. I could tell she liked Mrs DeWitt.

Now if only she could feel that way about her sons.

We walked inside. The DeWitts' living room was crammed with photos—baby pictures of Erick and Ryan and their proud, smiling parents; a younger Mrs DeWitt on stage, taking a bouquet of roses from Erick, in his dad's arms; the four of them on a mountain hike, at the zoo, on a ski slope and so on.

Stephie stopped to look at every one, her mouth open in awe.

In the kitchen, Erick and Ryan were wolfing down cream cheese sandwiches. With their free hands, they were reaching into a bag of crisps.

"Hey, you're taking mine!" Ryan shouted.

"There's plenty left," Erick shot back, grabbing a fistful of crisps. "It's a free country."

"Give me those!"

Ryan reached across the table, knocking the remaining crisps to the floor.

"Dawn, look what Ryan did," Erick said in a singsong voice.

"You telltale!"

"She saw you!"

I sighed. At last the mess was cleared up and we finished our snacks peacefully.

Then Erick decided he'd try to make

friends with Stephie. "Do you want to play Turtles?" he asked. "I'll be Leo and you be Raph."

"And I'm Don," Ryan added.

Stephie shook her head. "Uh-uh."

"OK," Erick said. "Er . . . how about hide and seek?"

"I don't want to play that either."

"Freeze tag?"

Stephie shook her head. "I can't play anything rough. I might get an asthma attack."

"Oh." Erick looked at her blankly.

"Come on, Leo," Ryan said. "*Cowabunga*, dude!"

The boys ran outside, off to . . . wherever Ninja Turtles go.

Now, Stephie's asthma no longer prevents her from running around. And anyway, it's usually emotional stress that triggers her attacks. Come to think of it, though, maybe running around with Erick and Ryan could be classified as emotional stress. So I wasn't going to drag Stephie outside. But I couldn't just ignore the DeWitt boys.

In a pile of things by the back door, I saw two bats and a ball. "I know," I said. "We can play bat and ball outside, just you and me."

Her eyes lit up. "OK!"

That worked terrifically—for about ten minutes. Then Erick insisted on playing. Before long, he and Ryan were trying to prove who could throw the fastest.

Well, when two boys have a throwing contest, you know what happens. Someone always gets hit on the head.

And you can guess who it was.

"Owwwww!" Stephie cried.

"It's only rubber," Erick said.

"Have we got to take her to the hostipal?" Ryan asked.

"*Hospital*, stupid!"

"I'm not stupid!"

"Calm down, boys!" I said.

Stephie was hugging me, whimpering.

Ryan walked closer to her, staring at her head. "Has she got a big bump?"

Immediately Stephie stuck her palm in front of his face.

Ryan's eyes widened. "*Nit protection?* I haven't got nits!"

"Yes, you have," Stephie said.

Erick was rolling on the ground, laughing. "Ryan's got nits!"

As for me, I was vowing to myself never, *ever* to double-book again.

It seemed like weeks before Mrs DeWitt got back. I don't know who was happier to see her, the boys or me.

We were in the playroom when she

bustled through the front door, carrying a large paper bag. "Anybody home?"

Erick, Ryan and Stephie all sprang to their feet. "Mum!" the boys screamed.

"What's in the bag?" Erick asked.

"Just some odds and ends for you boys." She put it down on the coffee table and started unloading it. "Socks, shoelaces, chewing gum. . ."

"Ooh, gum!" Erick squealed.

As he happily distributed the gum, I gave Mrs DeWitt a report on the afternoon. Out of the corner of my eye, I saw Stephie examining the shoelaces. She was fingering them as if they were jewellery.

That seemed rather odd, until I looked at her trainers. Her own laces were dirty, frayed, and full of knots.

A few moments later, we exchanged goodbyes, and Stephie and I left. For the first few minutes, she didn't say a word. At last I said, "Stephie, what's on your mind?"

"Mrs DeWitt should be *my* mum, not theirs!" she blurted out. "Then I would always get snacks and nice things, too."

"Joanna makes you snacks," I said. "And you could ask her or your dad to buy you some new laces."

Stephie nodded. "I know *that*. But if I had a mum, I wouldn't have to ask. She'd just buy them."

I sighed. I really love Stephie, and I'm glad that I've been able to do so much to help her.

But finding a mum was one area in which I was totally helpless.

8th
CHAPTER

Thursday hadn't been an easy day. I wanted so badly to relax, and just have a quiet family evening.

So what was sitting in the drive when I got home? Carol's car.

Big deal, I told myself. So the house would be a little loud. So Carol would want to know every detail about my day. So she'd laugh hysterically at Jeff's stupid jokes. It was OK. She had every right to be there. She was Dad's girlfriend. And I shouldn't be mean. After all, she *had* bought me that director's chair and the sunglasses and visor.

So why did I feel like heading right back to Stephie's?

Of course, I didn't do it. I put on a smile and walked inside.

Dad and Carol and Jeff were all in

the living room. Standing.

Dad was still wearing his suit and tie. Carol was wearing a dress, with a big, colourful beret on her red hair—and make-up, which is very unusual for her.

Behind them, I could see Mrs Bruen busily putting a meal on the dining room table. It looked like Thai food, which I love. Four places were set, with all our best china.

I looked on the bright side. At least we weren't having vegetable *chimichangas* again.

Jeff was nearly bursting with excitement. "Dad's going to make an announcement!" he said.

Oh, good, I thought. The last time something like this happened, I was in sixth grade and Dad had got a big promotion. (It was one of the last times I saw Mum and Dad happy together.)

"What's the news?" I asked.

A smile spread across Dad's face. He turned towards Carol. She grabbed his arm and planted a kiss on his cheek. "Go ahead, darling," she said. "You tell them."

I didn't like the sound of this.

"Well, Dawn, Jeff," Dad said. "You're about to have a stepmother."

I froze. The words floated around in my brain, falling apart into strange syllables.

For a moment I thought I'd heard wrong. Or I hadn't quite grasped the meaning.

"Dad and Carol are getting married!" Jeff shouted.

Thank you, Jeff. Now it was crystal clear.

And so was the huge diamond on Carol's new ring.

I could see Mrs Bruen watching me, looking for my reaction. Along with everyone else. I suddenly felt as if a giant magnifying glass had been put in front of me, and they were all peering through it.

I did the only thing I could do.

I bolted.

Between Jeff and Mrs Bruen, through the dining room, through the kitchen, down the hall, and into my room.

I slammed the door behind me.

My feet wouldn't stop moving. I paced up and down. I wanted to scream but my teeth were locked together.

This was wrong, wrong, wrong. They couldn't just decide like this. Not without at least *mentioning* it to me first. How long had they been planning this? Why had they kept it such a big secret from Jeff and me?

How dare they?

I decided to let them know how I felt. If I had to yell and scream and throw Thai food, I would make sure they knew how serious this was.

I grabbed the doorknob and yanked open the door.

The first thing I heard was Mrs Bruen's voice. "Poor dear. Is she all right?"

"Ohhhh, she's angry," Carol said, sounding shocked and hurt.

"No, not Dawn," Dad reassured her. "Not about this."

"Maybe she just wanted to change into something nice," Jeff suggested.

I took a deep breath. What was I doing? Was the big announcement really that surprising? Jeff and I both thought Dad might marry Carol. We'd talked about it. Dad had even dropped hints a couple of times.

Even *Stephie* and I had discussed it.

Still, hearing the news for real came as a shock. But I had to admit, that wasn't *their* fault. And it wasn't fair for me to storm away and ruin everyone's celebration.

You have no idea how hard it was to pull myself together. But I unclenched my teeth and walked back down the hall.

Dad and Carol watched me with shaky little smiles. Jeff was standing by the table, drooling over the food. Mrs Bruen was pottering around in the kitchen.

"Is everything OK?" Dad asked me, trying to sound cheerful.

Up, lips! I commanded. I felt my face

trying to smile. "Yes. I was just . . . taken by surprise, that's all. That's big news!"

Carol looked relieved. "Well, let's sit down." She angled her head towards the kitchen and said loudly enough for Mrs Bruen to hear, "Everything smells so fabulous!"

We gathered around the table and stood stiffly for a moment. I wondered if there were rules about this—who sits first at an engagement-announcement dinner?

Well, correct or not, Jeff made the first move. He plopped into his chair and spooned some curried noodles on to his plate. "Come on, I'm starving," he said.

The rest of us sat down. Dad produced a bottle of champagne and poured some for each of us (a very small amount for Jeff and me). Then he stood up and raised his glass high. "To the most beautiful family in the world—and its newest member."

"Hear, hear! There, there!" Jeff the Stand-up Comic cheered.

No, no, I wanted to say. But I didn't. I raised my glass and took a tiny sip.

Jeff gulped his down. "Yechh!" he said, breaking into a fit of coughing. Carol bolted up from her chair and began pounding him on the back.

"Ow! Stop!" Jeff protested.

"It's OK, Carol," Dad said with a smile. "As long as he's coughing he's all right."

Carol looked embarrassed. "I suppose I've got some things to learn about being a mother, haven't I?"

No comment.

Soon Jeff stopped coughing, and we ate. Well, three of us did. Carol seemed too excited. She talked instead. Non-stop.

OK, maybe I'm exaggerating. But she had hardly touched her plate by the time the rest of us were helping ourselves to seconds.

"So your dad tells me to dress up because we were going to a *basketball game*. Imagine! I mean, why *dress up* for that? So he picks me up, drives towards the stadium, and says, 'Let's get some coffee first.' He pulls up to this sweet little cafe—and the game's supposed to start in ten minutes. Well, little do I know he's going to propose. And on his knees! *Everyone* in the cafe is watching, and when I say yes, they start applauding, and the waiters break into song. It was so romantic. Oh, I was really blushing!"

"I would have gone to the game," Jeff remarked.

"Have you shown them the ring?" Dad asked Carol.

She held out her hand. The diamond was

surrounded by sapphires. "Isn't it *breath-taking*?" she said.

I, for one, was still breathing. "Beautiful," I replied.

Jeff glanced at it and shoved some shrimp with peanut sauce into his mouth.

Now that Carol was quiet for a moment, I decided to ask, "When's the wedding?"

"The sooner the better!" Carol said.

"We haven't decided," Dad added.

So there was still time!

Stop that, I said to myself. I couldn't believe how negative I was being. Dad looked happy, and that was the most important thing. Wasn't it?

Carol picked up her fork and began eating again. The rest of us were using chopsticks, even Jeff. We always did. It was a family tradition. I remembered how much fun we had learning to use them. Eating Thai food with a fork seemed, well, unnatural.

I tried to ignore that. It wasn't a big deal.

Then Jeff reached for some coriander chicken and knocked his glass of water on to the floor. "Uh-oh!" he said.

Carol shot out of her chair. She ran into the kitchen and came back with a handful of paper towels. "No problem," she said. She began wadding up the paper and trying to soak the water out of the carpet.

Well, first of all, Jeff is old enough to

clean up after himself. Second, it's so environmentally wasteful to use paper towels for a water spill. A dry sponge would have soaked it up perfectly well.

But no one seemed to mind. Dad and Jeff thanked her, and Carol marched proudly back to the kitchen to throw out her soggy portion of destroyed American forest.

After dinner, as we cleared the plates, Jeff asked, "What's for dessert?"

Carol and Dad shared a glance, and I knew something was up.

"You kids get strawberry shortcake," Dad said, "but your stepmum and I are going out to celebrate."

"*Again?*" Jeff said.

"Oh, sweetie," Carol said with a laugh, "it's not often a person gets engaged, you know."

Stepmum? Sweetie? I realized I was going to have to get used to some new words in the house.

And it looked as if I'd also have to get used to seeing less of my dad.

He and Carol left, laughing and chatting, arms around each other. I sat at the kitchen table with Jeff and ate about three strawberries.

"Full?" Jeff asked.

"Yes," I replied, standing up. "Excuse me. I've got lots of homework."

"There's no excuse for *you*!"

"Shut up, Jeff!" I snapped.

I cleared my plate, went straight to my room, and plopped down on my bed.

I'd tried my hardest. I'd been polite and friendly. I hadn't ruined the celebration.

But now what? Now Dad was getting married. Carol was going to be eating every meal with us. I'd be seeing her first thing in the morning, and she'd probably be kissing Jeff and me goodnight every night. She'd go shopping with us and take holidays with us.

And when I wanted to have a nice quiet talk with Dad, Carol would be there.

I realized something then. I hated her. There was no use pretending otherwise. Who did she think she was, barging in on our lives? She was a loud, obnoxious, teenage wannabe, and she didn't deserve someone like my father.

Then again, it took two to make an engagement.

I was gritting my teeth again. This wasn't what I'd had in mind when I came to live in California. I'd had to leave my other family, upset my friends, work hard to adjust to a new school—and for what? To spend six months with *Dad*. Couldn't he at least have waited till I went back to

Connecticut? I suppose he *preferred* to spend time with her.

One thing seemed clear. I wasn't wanted here.

But I *was* wanted somewhere else, by my mum and my stepsister and my best friends.

That was when I made my big decision. I was going to move back to Stoneybrook.

9th CHAPTER

"Jeff Schafer, get back in this house," I heard my dad call out.

"I can walk to school by myself!" Jeff retorted. "I'm *ten*!"

"No, you're not, you're Jeff." (Ooh, two points for Dad!) "And I'm your father, who makes the rules around here. *Dawn! Are you ready?*"

"Just a second!" I shouted back.

In my room, I scribbled furiously on a sheet of stationery. It was Friday, the morning after the wedding announcement. I had a little announcement of my own to make.

I wasn't going to make it aloud, and I certainly wasn't going to wait for dinner. By dinnertime I hoped to be high above the country, flying eastward.

Quickly I glanced over my note:

Dear Dad,

I won't be home from school because I'm on my way to Stoneybrook. But I'm sure you don't mind. Now you can spend as much time as you want with your future wife. You won't have a daughter around to cramp your style.

Good luck with your wedding plans. Tell Jeff I still love him. And don't be upset. I'll be with people who care about me.

Love, Dawn

It sounds sneaky, I know. But I had no choice. Can you imagine if I'd *asked* permission to skip school and fly to Connecticut? My mum would think I was crazy. As it was, getting her to let me leave Stoneybrook in mid-year had been like moving a boulder up a steep mountain.

Once I arrived in Stoneybrook, I'd explain what had happened, and she'd accept it. I was sure she would. I did have a home there, after all.

I folded up the note, put it in an envelope,

and stuffed it deep into my rucksack.

Then I put on the pack and grabbed the pen and another sheet of paper. Quickly I tiptoed into Dad's empty bedroom. His credit cards were strewn on the top of his chest of drawers. I copied the number of one card on to the paper and shoved it into my jeans pocket.

I felt really guilty about that. But it wasn't as if I were *stealing* Dad's money. He was going to have to pay for my flight back eventually, right?

I was ready.

My heart was beating like crazy. If I pulled this off, it would be a miracle.

I ran into the kitchen. Dad was standing at the table—tying his tie, drinking his coffee and reading the morning paper at the same time.

Probably thinking about Carol, too.

"Sorry I took so long," I said, "but I wanted to tidy up because today's Mrs Bruen's day off . . . isn't it?"

Dad glanced up for a minute and frowned thoughtfully. "Friday . . . you're right, it is."

Good. I'd just wanted to make sure. Now my plan was set!

Phase One: The Preparation. Walk to school as if nothing were wrong.

"Well, 'bye, Dad!" I called out.

"So long, Sunshine!" he replied.

Sunshine. Ugh! I wondered what nickname he was going to give Carol. Motormouth?

Jeff pushed open the front door. "Come on, *Sunslime.*"

"You're so funny I forgot to laugh," I answered. I couldn't be too angry with him, though. This was the last we'd be seeing of each other for a while. Obnoxious as he was, I was going to miss Jeff.

Halfway to school, Jeff left me to walk with some friends. I felt a tug inside. He was going to be so furious with me for leaving unexpectedly. I wanted to give him a big hug and a kiss goodbye, but not in front of his friends. He'd never let me forget it.

Eventually I met up with Sunny and Maggie. I was *dying* to tell them my secret. But I couldn't. It would be too painful to see their reactions.

As we neared school, Sunny and Maggie were laughing about my description of Thursday's sitting job. And looking into their faces, I began to have cold feet. Would they forgive me? How could the W ♥ KC possibly survive now with only three members?

I thought about staying. Then I imagined what it would be like to come home from school and be greeted at the door by Carol. That was all it took. I was ready for Phase Two of my plan: Dawn's Acting Audition.

I stopped walking. "Ugh! My stomach."

"Are you OK?" Sunny asked.

"Yeah." I walked a few more steps, then grimaced. "Owww, what a cramp. Must have been the shrimp omelette I ate this morning."

Shrimp omelette? I don't know how I thought of that. But it worked. Sunny and Maggie both nodded.

"Dawn, you shouldn't be at school today," Maggie said.

Sunny took my arm. "I'll walk you home."

Uh-oh! That wasn't part of the plan. "No, you'll be late. I'll be fine."

"Are you sure?" Maggie asked.

"Uh-huh. I just need to lie down. I'll . . . see you later."

"OK. . ." Sunny said reluctantly.

"We'll tell your tutor, so don't worry," Maggie assured me.

"Thanks," I replied. "'Bye!"

"Hope you feel better soon!"

I felt *awful* lying to them. As soon as they were out of sight, I checked my watch. It was eight-thirty, and Dad would be rushing out of the house.

By the time I reached our house, his car had gone. I let myself in the front door.

Phase Three: The Getaway.

I dropped my bag and pulled the credit card number out of my pocket. Then I went to the kitchen and leafed through the *Yellow Pages*.

Being bi-coastal, I know all the airlines that fly to Connecticut. I began phoning them.

I was on the phone for half an hour (mostly on hold). The first airline I reached had a seat on Tuesday. The second was booked solid for the next week.

But the operator at the third one said, "I'm showing a cancellation for two seats, but it's a three o'clock flight this afternoon. And it leaves from LAX, not John Wayne. Is that all right?"

John Wayne Airport is close to our house. LAX is Los Angeles International Airport, which is nearly an hour away.

"Fine!" I cried. "I'll take one seat."

I read her my dad's credit card number. Then she mentioned the price.

I almost fainted.

But hey, if I left a few months later the flight might cost *more*. Prices tend to go up over time, so I was actually doing Dad a favour.

At least that was what I told myself.

I wrote down the information and rang off. Then I pulled my goodbye note out of my rucksack and added a couple of lines:

P.S. My flight arrives in Connecticut at 11:00 tonight, their time. I'll call Mum from the airport.

'Bye!

I left the note on the kitchen table. Then I raced into my room, grabbed a shoulder bag from my wardrobe, and began to pack.

It didn't take long. I wouldn't be needing my light California outfits in Stoneybrook. I'd left all my heavy winter clothes there, anyway.

I made sure to take my journal, a few photos of Jeff and Dad, and my copies of the W ♥ KC article and video. I stuffed every last penny of my babysitting money into my pocket.

At nine forty-five I looked through the *Yellow Pages* again and called a taxi. When it arrived, I raced outside as fast as I could, wearing a wide-brimmed hat. (The last thing I needed was for some neighbour to see me and phone my dad.)

I climbed in, slammed the door, and ducked below the window. The driver pulled away, and Phase Four began: Dawn's Trip Home.

You wouldn't believe how much it costs to take a taxi from Palo City to Los Angeles! I nearly died.

Nearly all my babysitting money went into that ride. I had enough left to buy one bag of nuts, which had to last me for three and a half hours while I waited for my flight.

But that was OK. I wouldn't need any money on the plane. And afterwards, I'd be in Connecticut!

I kept thinking I could see familiar faces in the airport. I was petrified someone would recognize me. Under my wide hat, I began to feel like an international spy. A young guy on his way to Cleveland sat next to me for a while. When he asked my name, I told him it was Mariso Van Raymond. I even tried to use an exotic accent.

At two forty-five I boarded. For the first hour of the flight, I could hardly sit still. I wanted to scream out my secret to everybody—I, Dawn Schafer, had left school, booked my own flight and taken a taxi to L.A. By myself.

And it was so *easy*. I've never felt so independent in my life.

My exhilaration lasted till dinner. Some-where over Nebraska, reality began to set in.

Maybe it was the wilted salad, or the tasteless roll. Or the fact that there weren't any vegetarian meals left so I had to share my flight with part of an overcooked chicken carcass.

Whatever it was, dread started creeping through me. It was about five-thirty, California time, and Dad would be coming home. I imagined his and Jeff's expressions when they saw the note. Then I pictured how Sunny and the other girls would react when they found out.

They would feel horrified. Disappointed. Betrayed.

What had I done? I'd never dreamed of skipping school to go to the cinema, let alone to board a cross-country jet and charge it to my dad. It was insane.

Suddenly, two thousand miles away, I felt pretty stupid.

I was a criminal. I was a runaway. I had stolen money from my own father. I would step off the plane into a circle of policemen with handcuffs. Rhonda Lieb would call me "the W ♥ KC fugitive" in the paper. Chuck Raymond would interview Sunny, who'd hardly be able to speak through her tears.

My eyes began to close over Indiana, and

I slept too deeply for my worries to turn into nightmares.

I woke up to the sound of the flight captain saying, "We are now beginning the descent to our final destination. The weather in Connecticut is cold and clear, about twenty-eight degrees. There's a fresh coat of snow on the ground, but the runway is completely dry."

Snow! I'd almost forgotten what that was like. I began to feel excited again. Soon I'd be hugging Mary Anne. We'd stay up all night talking. I'd wake her tomorrow morning to build a snowman.

I was fluttery all over as the plane landed. I rushed to the exit. As I neared the end of the ramp, I scanned the terminal for a pay phone.

But I didn't need one. Mum was waiting for me at the gate.

And her expression could have burned a hole through sheet metal.

10th CHAPTER

Saturday

Dear Dawn,

It seems silly to be writing this to you now. I mean, we just spent the whole day together talking. (Well, most of the day.) I'm so sorry about what happened.

I hope things aren't going too terribly right now. I've thought a lot about your problem. I can imagine how you feel. I mean, it *was hard for me when my dad got married, even though I liked your mum so much.*

Anyway, don't worry. We all love you. I just thought you should know that...

I got Mary Anne's letter on Wednesday. It was so nice to see some sympathetic words for a change. The weather may have been in the 70s and 80s, but it felt really frosty in my dad's house.

Yes, I was back in Palo City. Needless to say, my trip to Stoneybrook didn't work out. (*That* is an understatement!)

Let me begin at the beginning. First of all, I was shocked when I saw Mum at the airport. I wanted to run to her and hug her, but the look on her face stopped me.

"Hi!" I said. "How did you know I was coming?"

The Mask of Doom opened her mouth. "How do you think I knew? Your father rang me two hours ago."

"Oh," I said. "He found the note."

"Yes, he did. And he was in a panic. He spent an hour on the phone calling every airline on the West Coast. Then he thought you might have hitchhiked to the airport, so he contacted the police. When he phoned me, he could hardly speak. I could hear Jeff in the background, crying."

I could tell Mum was trying very hard not to scream at me. Her head looked as though it were vibrating. I'd never seen her like this.

"Sorry," I said, gazing at the floor.

"You'd better be. How could you have done this, Dawn Schafer? How could you be so irresponsible and immature? Not to mention *deceitful*. Do you *know* what you put your family through? After all we did so you could move to California for six months, all the adjustments we made, all the emotional strain? And you just up and booked a flight on your father's credit card for the fun of it? What on earth could have possessed you to do something like this?"

Tears welled up in my eyes. "It wasn't . . . for the fun of it," I managed to say.

Mum pointed to a nearby chair. "I brought your coat. Put it on while I phone your dad to let him know you got here safely. He's worried sick, and he feels responsible. We'll talk more on the way home."

My down coat was lying on the chair. That was a good sign. At least Mum wasn't going to let me freeze.

I watched my mother make her call on a pay phone. I could hear Dad's voice booming from the other end. He didn't sound happy. Luckily Mum didn't make me speak to him.

Then she and I walked silently to the car park and found her car. Neither of us said a word until we were on the motorway, heading home.

I tried to explain my feelings about Carol and Dad. As the words came out of my mouth, they sounded shallow and stupid.

But Mum listened carefully. She hadn't known about the engagement, and I think the news shook her up a little, too. Slowly the smoke coming from her ears began to clear away.

"Did you tell Dad how you felt?" she asked.

"No," I said. "I was too angry."

"So you ran away from the situation."

"I suppose so."

"Here's what I don't understand, Dawn. You honestly thought we wouldn't mind? You thought you could just change your plans and it would affect nobody but yourself?"

"Mum, I—I just wasn't thinking about all that. I was upset."

"I can see that. But now quite a few people are upset. Including your dad. You're going to have a lot to work out with him. Starting with that plane ticket."

"I'll pay him back out of my babysitting money, I promise. No matter how long it takes. Everyone in the BSC has told me they're incredibly busy."

"Darling, it's going to take longer than you think. First of all, you're going to have to repay him for *two* tickets. And second of all, you're going to be doing it in California."

I stared at her. "*What?*"

"I've booked a flight back for you. It leaves tomorrow afternoon at four o'clock. Don't forget, you still have some time left on your six months, Dawn."

"But—but—don't you want me to stay?"

Mum sighed. Her voice softened. "Of course I do. But not under these conditions. If you're ready to come home, you need to make a plan that includes all of us."

I slumped into my seat. Part of me understood what she was saying. I shouldn't have been so selfish. But nobody was seeing *my* point of view. First Dad had crowded me out of his life, and now Mum was sending me away, too. (Funny how she got worked up over the ticket I'd charged, but it was no problem spending the money to send me back.) Wasn't I important to *anybody*?

We arrived home after midnight. Richard and Mary Anne had already gone to sleep. I crept upstairs to my room.

Everything was just as I'd left it. It looked so comfortable and homey. As I threw my rucksack on my bed, I noticed a folded-up note there.

I picked it up and read:

Dear Dawn,

If I fell asleep before you got home, I'm sorry. I'm sure you've been yelled at enough by now, so I won't ask questions like why did you do it. I'm just glad tomorrow is Saturday so we can actually talk to each other in person!

We might as well make the most of

our few hours together, huh?

Welcome home.
Love, your sister,
Mary Anne

It was the nicest thing I'd seen all day. Trust Mary Anne! For the first time since I'd got off the plane, my mixed-up feelings came pouring out. Anger at Carol, anger *and* love for Dad, love for Mary Anne, hurt at my mother's reaction, shame for what I'd done . . . they were all so powerful and bewildering.

I buried my face in my pillow and cried my heart out.

The next thing I knew, someone was knocking at my door.

I struggled to open my eyes. It was light outside. My bedside table clock said 7:09. But my watch said 4:09, and so did my California-conditioned body.

"Come in," I croaked.

The door burst open. "Hi!"

Mary Anne ran in and jumped on my bed. She was still wearing her nightie, but she looked refreshed and excited.

Me? I felt as if I'd been run over by a steam-roller, but it was so good to see Mary Anne.

"I know, I'm not supposed to be nice to you," she said. "But I'm *so* happy you're home!"

I sat up and gave her a hug. Both of us burst into tears.

Over Mary Anne's shoulder, I saw Mum peering into the room. She was trying to look stern, but I could detect a trace of a smile. "Dawn," she said. "Richard's making breakfast downstairs. You and Mary Anne can hang around the house till your flight, but you are not to call any of your friends while you're here. Is that understood?"

I nodded.

As soon as Mum left, Mary Anne pulled away from me, found a tissue, and blew her nose. Then she drew in a deep breath and said, "Tell me *everything*!"

So I did. At least I tried to. Our conversation bounced all over the place.

At one point Mary Anne mentioned the Kristy crisis. "Did you get my letter about Kristy's latest scheme?"

"Well, I know she phoned the TV station—"

"She went further than that. I couldn't believe it. We'd all decided we didn't need more publicity. But in one of our meetings—just one—we didn't get any calls from clients. We started joking about how we *should* try to get on TV."

"And Kristy didn't think it was a joke," I guessed.

"That's right. She actually sent her copy of the We Love Kids Club video to the TV station. She enclosed a letter that said something like, 'They were big in California, but they're even better in Connecticut!' The problem was, she forgot to rewind the tape. So the TV people put it on and saw a commercial for indestructible pantyhose."

"No!"

"Yes. They thanked Kristy and sent back the tape with a list of advertising fees."

We cracked up.

Well, Mary Anne and I chatted while we got dressed, chatted over breakfast, and didn't stop chatting all day.

The afternoon arrived much faster than I'd expected. Mum drove me back to the airport. Our journey there was almost as grim as the one home had been the night before.

We did hug and kiss goodbye, though. And Mum had tears in her eyes when I left.

The flight took off on time, and I braced myself for what would happen when I saw Dad.

And Carol.

11th CHAPTER

Ohio hadn't changed. Neither had Kansas. Nor Minnesota. In fact, the country looked exactly the same as it had the day before.

Luckily I didn't have to deal with a lump of dead flesh in my meal on the return flight. *This* airline had a reasonable meat-less lasagne.

It didn't matter. I had no appetite. Besides, I might have a second chance later. For all I knew, Dad had another ticket back to Connecticut lined up for me. I could see myself becoming a human tennis ball, going to and fro, to and fro across the country. Maybe I could notch up enough Frequent Flyer miles to take a free trip to China. Then neither Mum nor Dad would have to see me.

Dad was waiting at the airport. I noticed

he didn't have a ticket in his hand (phew!) But he did have the same disgusted and angry expression on his face that Mum had had.

And he was ready with most of the same words, too. Once again I heard *selfish, immature* and *irresponsible*. I had to give Dad points for originality, though. He also came up with *underhanded, spoiled* and *reckless.*

Then came the ritual of driving home. I wasn't looking forward to that. My flight had come into LAX again, and it was going to be a long ride to Palo City.

But Dad surprised me. When he'd finished his lecture, he said, "Dawn, I know something is bothering you terribly. And I am your father. If you need to tell me anything, I'm all ears."

"You mean, you're not angry?" I asked.

"I didn't say *that*!" Dad scowled, but then he actually broke into a smile.

Hallelujah! I felt as if I'd emerged from a swamp and into the sunlight.

"Well, to tell you the truth" (I took a deep breath), "this has to do with you and Carol."

Dad sighed. "I can't say I'm surprised. Go on."

I told him how I felt about Carol. I listed her habits that bothered me. I mentioned how hurt I'd felt when they'd announced their engagement.

Dad listened intently. When I'd finished, he shook his head and said, "I had no idea, Dawn. I thought you and Carol had worked out your problems. Why didn't you tell me things had gone off track?"

"She's your *girlfriend*, Dad. I didn't want to hurt your feelings. Besides, she's not a bad person. And you seemed to be happy with her. I *was* trying hard to like her. But when I realized she was going to marry you and become my stepmum, everything just sort of exploded."

"So you thought I'd betrayed you, and you wanted to get back at me."

"No, I thought you didn't want me around."

"Oh, Sunshine, how could you think that? You know that's not true."

"It turned out *Mum* was the one who didn't want me," I said, staring out of the window. "She'd bought my return ticket before I'd even landed. I was so stupid!"

"It wasn't that she didn't want you, Dawn. She's dying for you to go back to Connecticut. But she and I both feel you need to learn to live up to your commitments. Moving out here was a big decision, not something you can change on a whim."

103

For about the tenth time in twenty-four hours, I was getting choked up. "OK," I murmured.

Dad gave me a quick glance, then turned back to the road. When he spoke, his voice was gentle. "Being a divorced kid isn't easy, is it?"

"Nope," was the only word I could manage, between sniffles.

It was about 7:15, California time, when we arrived home. As we pulled into the drive, Jeff ran out of the house.

"Hi, Dawn!" he said. "Are you OK?"

"Yes," I replied.

"How did you *do* it? Like, buying the ticket and going to the airport and all? That's so cool!"

"Don't even *think* about it!" Dad called from the driver's seat.

Jeff and I walked to the front door together. "Did you do it because of Dad and Carol?" he asked.

I nodded.

"I don't blame you," he whispered. "If you'd told me, I would have gone with you."

I smiled at my brother. I was glad to see the real Jeff emerge from behind the joke machine for a change.

As we walked inside, Mrs Bruen ran to

me and gave me a big hug. "Welcome home, dear," she said.

More waterworks.

Eventually I went to my room, followed by my brother. I could tell he'd been afraid, and he didn't want to let me out of his sight.

He shut the door behind him and plopped down on my bed. "Dawn," he said, his voice hardly audible, "did Dad tell you about his argument with Carol?"

"No." I sat down next to him. "What happened?"

"Well, she came over last night when Dad was screaming at Mum on the phone. So she and I played seven games of draughts, and I won five. When Dad got off the phone he told Carol what you'd done. She said, 'I'll stay and help,' and Dad said, 'No, I think you'd better go home,' and Carol got all upset. She said, 'If I go home I'll just worry. Please, I'm going to be part of the family, remember?' He said, 'Yes, I remember, but that's not the point now. This is something important that I need to work out with Dawn and her mother.' And she said, 'I know, I know, there'll always be something more important than me.' Then Dad blew up. He called her selfish."

That sounded familiar.

"And she *cried*," Jeff went on. "And you know what else? On the way out, she threw her engagement ring on the floor."

"So it's off?"

Jeff looked puzzled. "Yes, I said she *threw* it."

"No, I mean the engagement."

"No. They talked on the phone later, and it sounded as if the fight was over. But Dad has to repair the ring."

Wow! I'd never seen Dad and Carol angry with one another. Maybe their relationship wasn't perfect after all.

Later on, when I was alone in my room, I heard Carol come in the front door. She and Dad talked for a few minutes. Then I heard a knock on my door.

"Mind if I come in?" Carol's voice said.

"No," I replied.

She stepped in, looking worried. As she shut the door behind her, she said, "I'm glad you're back. Are you too tired to have a little talk?"

I felt completely talked out. I wanted to tell her to come back the next day.

But if I turned her away, Dad would probably be angry, and that was the last thing I wanted.

Besides, I was feeling guilty. I'd rejected

Carol, but she wasn't the real reason for my anger. I'd been feeling rejected by Dad. He could have got engaged to *anybody*, and I'd probably have felt the same way.

"I'm not too tired," I said.

Carol sat down on the bed. She was smiling, but she looked stiff and nervous. "So, how was . . . your flight?"

I didn't want to beat about the bush. "Carol, I'm sorry about what I did. This is supposed to be a happy time for you and Dad, and I'm spoiling it for you."

"I was worried that—" She shifted uncomfortably. "You know, that you didn't want us to get married."

"Don't worry about that, Carol. The problem has more to do with me. I really am glad you and Dad are engaged. I mean, it did come as a shock, and I didn't exactly know what to say. Or how to act." I looked her in the eye and tried to smile. "But I know how happy my dad is. He really loves you."

Carol's eyes filled. She opened her arms and we shared a hug.

The last thing she said before she left was, "Friends?"

I forced a smile. "Yes. Friends."

I went to bed immediately afterwards, but I was too exhausted to fall asleep straight away. For a few minutes I just lay there, relieved that the talk with Carol was over. Maybe now I could put my nightmare behind me, prepare for the wedding, and work like crazy to pay back those plane tickets.

Which meant I'd be babysitting till I was ninety.

12th CHAPTER

Saturday

Dear Dawn,

Hi! I got your letter today while Jessi and I were baby-sitting.

Mal's allowed to sit again. She's still a little weak, but she's almost totally better.

Dawn, I CAN'T BELIEVE YOU WERE ACTUALLY IN THE SAME TOWN AS US!

You should have called.

Stop, Jessi! (She's kidding, Dawn.) Anyway, we laughed at the part of the letter about Jeff — how he's been calling you names all this time, and then he cried after you'd left.

*It was as if
you were describing
our sitting job.*

Whew. After today I may have to
go back to bed...

Mallory was up and around now, but her
parents weren't letting her take part in
after-school activities or go on sitting jobs.
But she could go to school and babysit at her
own house—as long as she took it easy.

Unfortunately, taking it easy and sitting
for the Pikes is like keeping dry in the
shower. Impossible.

As I mentioned before, Mal has *seven*
younger siblings. The oldest are ten-year-
old triplets called Adam, Jordan and
Byron. Then there's Vanessa (who's nine);
Nicky (eight); Margo (seven); and Claire
(five).

It takes at least two to sit for the Pikes,
usually one BSC member plus Mallory.
Lately, though, two seems too few: the
triplets have decided they're old enough
now to do whatever they want.

On that dreary winter Saturday, they
were making a secret potion in the basement. Vanessa the Dragon was hiding from

Claire the Knight, and Margo and Nicky were playing draughts in the living room.

Jessi and Mal were in the kitchen, making lunch.

"Where is she?" Claire asked, rushing into the kitchen. She was brandishing a toy ray gun and wearing a cape made from an old shirt.

"I thought you were a knight," Jessi said, looking at the gun.

"A space knight, you silly-billy-goo-goo," Claire answered.

Oh. Of course.

Claire disappeared upstairs and into a bedroom.

"RAAAUUUUUURRRGHHHH!" Vanessa was a pretty convincing dragon.

"Aaaaaargh!" Claire ran back into the kitchen, giggling, with Vanessa in pursuit.

"You woke me up behind the bed. Now I shall eat your little head!" Vanessa howled. (She loves speaking in rhyme. It drives everyone crazy.)

From the living room, Margo yelled, "I win again!"

"But I haven't moved yet!" Nicky protested.

"You can't, doofus," Margo replied. "You're trapped! New game!"

"I hate this!" Nicky said.

"UGHHHHHHH!" floated up from the basement, followed by wild laughter.

Jessi and Mal exchanged a Look. "I'll go this time," Mal said with a sigh.

She trudged downstairs. "OK, you lot, what are you doing?"

The boys were clustered around a big sink next to Mr Pike's workbench. "Get out!" Adam said.

Mal ignored him. She moved closer and saw a bucket in the sink. Inside the bucket was a disgusting brown liquid—and the Pikes' hamster, Frodo, sloshing around in total confusion.

"What *is* this?" Mallory asked.

"It's a formula," Jordan said.

"We're making a secret growth serum and we want to see if it works," Byron added. "But Frodo won't drink it."

On a nearby worktop, Mal could see a small carton of milk, a bag of potting compost, some marshmallows, butterscotch syrup, baking powder, wadded-up lint from the clothes dryer, a pile of sawdust and some glue. The secret ingredients.

"Boys, this is ridiculous," Mal said. "Get Frodo out of there and wash him."

Adam shook his head and sighed. "You're getting in the way of science!"

"It's all right," Jordan said. He didn't drink any of the potion, but he's covered

112

with it. I think that'll work. We can put him in the cage and monitor his growth."

The boys began arguing over who would have to lift the poor animal out, and Mal went back upstairs. She bumped into Nicky, who was on his way down. "Can I play?" he asked his brothers.

"No!" they shouted at once. Adam added, "You have to be ten to join the science club."

"No, you don't!" Nicky yelled. "You started it when you were nine."

"At least we haven't got bad breath!" Byron shot back.

"*Byron!*" exclaimed Mallory.

"It's true!" Adam said. "He smells like sardines."

"I *like* sardines!" Nicky protested.

"Ugh!" moaned the creators of the growth serum.

Nicky stormed upstairs.

Mal went back to lunch duty. Before long, she and Jessi had put together a pile of sandwiches, and they called the other kids into the kitchen.

You should see lunch at Mallory's house. It's not exactly elegant dining. Kristy calls it "Pikes at Trough".

The kids bolted their lunch in seconds. Afterward the triplets went into the hall and began putting on their coats.

"Er, where are you boys going?" Jessi asked.

"To Carle Playground," Adam replied.

"Hmmm, did they ask *you* for permission, Jessi?" Mal inquired.

"No," Jessi answered innocently. "Did they ask you?"

The triplets looked at each other and rolled their eyes. "Can we go?" Byron grunted.

"It's cold and yucky out, and it looks like rain or snow," Mal said.

"So?" Jordan replied. "We're not going *for ever*."

"I'll go with you," Nicky volunteered.

"Oh, great," Byron muttered.

"No way, Nicky-Nicky-breath-so-icky," Adam chanted.

"*Adam!*" Mallory exclaimed.

"He always gets in the way," Jordan said.

"No, I don't!" Nicky snapped, his eyes brimming with tears.

"Besides, he might think the fish in the pond are sardines and eat them!" Jordan cracked up at his own joke.

"Come on, let's go," Adam said as they headed for the door.

Nicky ran after them, his face bright red. He held the door open and yelled, "Good riddance! I didn't want to play with you puke-heads anyway!"

He slammed the door and ran back through the kitchen. Mal and Jessi felt awful for him. "Nicky?" Mal said.

"I wish they were *dead*!" was Nicky's reply.

"Be careful what you wish for, it might come true!" Vanessa called from inside the living room.

"Good!" Nicky ran to his room and slammed *that* door.

Mal waited a moment, then climbed the stairs and knocked gently on the door. "Are you OK?"

"I'm *so* happy they've gone," he said. "I hope they never come back."

"Well, if you need to talk, I'll be downstairs with Jessi."

Nicky murmured something, and Mal went back to the kitchen, where she and Jessi were clearing up.

Apparently Nicky recovered. A few minutes later he'd sneaked down to the living room and was whooping about how he was going to "demolish" Vanessa at draughts.

About half an hour later, at 1:00, it began to rain. "Ha!" Nicky's voice floated in from the living room. "Now they're going to get wet and freeze!"

The rain fell harder. The house got so

dark that Jessi and Mal had to turn lights on. Then the wind began rattling the windows. Eventually Nicky wandered into the kitchen. "Are they back yet?" he asked.

"No," Jessi replied.

Mal looked at the oven clock, which said 1:37. "Hmm, they've been out there quite a while. I hope they're OK."

Nicky's brow was furrowed. "Maybe something's happened to them."

"No, they can take care of themselves," Mal said.

Nicky left, then came back a moment later. "How cold does it have to be to get frostbite?" he asked.

"Cold enough to snow, I think," Jessi replied. "Why?"

"They didn't take their waterproof gloves."

Mal raised her eyebrows. "Are you *worried* about your brothers, Nicky?"

"No way!"

Five minutes later thunder began to boom. "Uh-oh! Where are they?" Mallory murmured.

Nicky ran into the kitchen, looking worried. "Let's phone the police," he suggested. "What if a tree fell on them, or they got hit by lightning?"

Mal sighed. "They should know it's

dangerous to be out in weather like this."

"Yes!" Nicky was on the verge of tears now.

"I could go and look for them," Jessi said.

Nicky ran to get his coat. "I'll go with you!"

Whack!

The back door slammed open. Adam, Byron and Jordan tumbled inside. They were panting and laughing, out of breath, and their footsteps made loud squishy noises on the floor.

"Made it!" Adam said.

The boys were sopping wet from head to toe. Their coats and shoes were two shades darker than before, and their hair was matted against their heads.

"What happened?" Mal demanded.

"We tried to come back when the rain started, but it was too heavy," Adam said, "so we went inside the toolshed at the park, to wait it out. But the storm just got worse, so we ran for it!"

"It was *great*!" Jordan said with a laugh.

Mal and Jessi were relieved. Nicky? Well, he hugged and kissed them and told them how much he'd worried.

Just kidding.

His worried look had already twisted into

a sneer. "You're *ten*, and you're too stupid to come in and out of the rain?" he said.

"Go and wash your head in bubblegum," Adam replied.

"You look like *you* already did, greasehead!" Nicky snapped.

"Baby!" Byron said.

"Three Stooges!"

Ah, brotherly love!

13th CHAPTER

"Mm, great sesame noodles," Dad said. "Pass the soy sauce."

Carol quietly passed it, chewing on her sauteed vegetables.

The table fell silent. I could hear the bean sprouts crunching between my teeth.

"Knock-knock!" Jeff called out.

"Who's there?" Dad asked.

"Yeah."

"Yeah who?"

"What are you so happy about? *Get it?*"

I groaned. Dad laughed. Carol smiled and ate some more vegetables.

Silence again. My stomach growled. I felt as if we were eating dinner in a library.

For the first time in my life, I hoped Jeff would tell another daft joke. He seemed to be the only one who wasn't tense.

The house hadn't been the same since I'd

come back from Stoneybrook. Dad wasn't his usual happy-go-lucky self. One morning he went into a fit when a shoelace broke. Another time he shattered a coffee pot trying to jam it in the dishwasher, then walked off in a huff.

Things were worse when Carol came over. True, she no longer went overboard trying to be cool and talk like a teenager. Now she was going overboard in the *other* direction. She hardly ever spoke. She'd sit at the dinner table looking nervously at Dad and me like a school kid waiting to be punished in the head's office.

She was driving me crazy.

And it was all my fault. The more I thought about it, the more childish and ridiculous my plane trip seemed. If I'd just bothered to *talk* to Dad, I would have realized he wasn't rejecting me. But Dad and I weren't the only ones affected by my trip. How would *I* have felt if I were Carol, and my fiancé's daughter had run away from home after I'd announced my engagement? Awful. I would *never* forget it.

Despite our talk, I knew Carol wouldn't either. She couldn't walk into the house without feeling unwanted.

Which didn't make for lively dinners, that's for sure.

Explaining my trip to my friends was no

picnic, either. I spent the whole of a W ♥ KC meeting doing it. Sunny, Maggie and Jill were all sympathetic, but I could tell they couldn't *quite* understand it. Maggie seemed annoyed that I'd faked illness on the way to school that fateful day. The other girls just kept looking at me as if I'd gone slightly looney.

Mainly, though, I think they were relieved that I was back. Jobs were still coming in like crazy, and they couldn't afford to lose a member.

By the way, Sunny *had* bought a new calendar in time for that meeting. Unfortunately it didn't help much. By the time we'd finished talking about me, it was dinnertime.

Calls kept coming in to all our numbers. Sunny ended up double-booking herself again. She called me in a panic, and I agreed to take one of her jobs, sitting for Erick and Ryan at four-thirty on a Tuesday afternoon. That same day, though, I was already hired to walk Stephie home from school and sit for her until Joanna came back from the dentist. But Joanna had assured me she'd be back by 3:45, so it seemed okay.

Stephie was thrilled when I turned up outside her school that day. She held my hand and we swung arms, walking through the playground. "Dawn, I wrote a story today. I'm going to make it into a book. I'm going to illustrate it, too. And you know who I'm going to dedicate it to? *You!*"

"Oh, Stephie. That's so sweet," I said.

"Hi, Stephie!" a girl called from behind us.

We turned to see a pretty black-haired girl walking towards us with her mum. "Hi, Becky," Stephie replied.

"Who's that?" Becky asked, pointing at me.

Stephie hugged my arm and said, "That's my mummy."

"No, it's not," Becky said.

Her mum winked at me. "That's the youngest-looking mum *I've* ever seen. What's your secret?"

She and I laughed, talked a bit, and said goodbye. On the way home, Stephie and I passed a corner shop. "Ooh, can I get a treat?" she asked. "Please?"

"Stephie. . ."

"Then you won't have to make me an after-school snack."

She had a point. I was going to have to leave just a few minutes after I reached her house. "Oh, all right," I said. "But nothing too sweet."

"Great! I love when you buy me things, Dawn."

I bought her a bag of crisps and we

walked home contentedly.

We arrived there at 3.30. As soon as we were inside, Stephie insisted on showing me her story. I unfolded it and read:

The Special Flower
    by Stephanie Robertson

Once upon a time there was a very special flower in front of a wite house. A prety girl lived in there, and one day she was very sad. She ran outside, crying, "Boohoo" She layed down next to the flower.

The flower said "Why are you cryng" and the girl said "Because I dont have a mummy. She's dead."

But the flower just smiled. "Go to sleep and dont you wury. I am your mummy."

Well, the girl got angry. She said "No your not! your a flower. My mummy was berried in the ground!"

But the flower just smiled again. "Your right,"

she said, "but what ever is planted in the ground grows into something beautifull, doesn't it?"

The girl smiled back at the flower. And you know what? She was never sad again.

The End!

"Stephie, that's so . . . moving," I said.

It was too. I could hardly keep from "crying" myself.

Stephie said, "The flower's name is Dawn."

I didn't know what to say to *that*. Luckily Stephie ran into the playroom with her story then. "I'm going to start illustrating."

Well, 3:45 came and went. I began to feel nervous. At 4:05 the phone rang.

I picked up the receiver. "Hello, Robertson residence!"

"Hurro, dhaw?" said a weird, thick voice.

"Hello?"

"Icksh Showah-uh."

I decided it was a crank call, and I was about to hang up. Then I remembered Joanna was at the dentist. The last time my dad had gone to the dentist, he could hardly move his mouth afterwards. "Is that Joanna?" I asked.

"Uh-huh! Uh-huh!"

"Er, are you calling to say you'll be late?"

"Uh-huh!"

"Have you finished there?"

"Uh-huh!"

"So I'll see you soon?"

"Uh-huh!"

"OK, thanks! 'Bye!"

Oh, boy! At my fastest, I'd need ten minutes or so to get to the DeWitts'. I began pacing up and down. I wished Sunny hadn't double-booked herself. I vowed to organize the We ♥ Kids Club somehow.

Joanna arrived at 4:14 and gestured for me to leave. As I bustled out of the door, Stephie ran into the living room, looking crushed. "Do you *have* to go and babysit for those nit-heads?" she said. "I want to show you my illustrations."

"Sorry, Stephie," I replied. "I'll come over tomorrow, OK?"

"Yeah. 'Bye."

I felt really rotten.

At least I had plenty to think about on my run to the DeWitts'. Did Stephie really want *me*, or did she want someone to be her mummy? Funny, she wouldn't mind sharing her dad if he were to get married, but she had a hard time sharing me.

I had to admit, I knew how she felt. I certainly hadn't wanted to share my dad with Carol. And I completely screwed up my personal life to prove it.

Stephie was lucky, in a way. She was too young to let her jealousy make her do something seriously stupid, the way I had.

Then my thinking shifted. (Maybe all the running had shaken something loose in my brain.) *Ease up, Schafer,* I told myself. I was acting as if I'd committed the worst crime in the world. I wasn't the only person who ever felt jealous. Other people did stupid things, too, and it was easy to forgive them.

I thought of Kristy trying to get the BSC on TV. I don't know if she'll *ever* recover from the fact that the W ♥ KC "made it" first. I don't know if she'll ever get over her resentment of me. But I love her anyway.

Come to think of it, Jeff could be an unbelievable pain to me, and I still love him. And if Nicky Pike could still have feelings for those three monsters in his house. . .

It's all so mixed up. You resent people you love (like Nicky and his brothers), you love people who resent you (me and Kristy), you resent people who love people you love (me and Carol), you resent not having someone to love (Stephie and her imaginary mum), and you think people who love you resent you (me and Dad, or me and Mum).

Feelings are weird. I don't think I'll ever completely understand them.

As I approached the DeWitts' house, with three minutes to spare, I slowed to walk. I wanted a glass of water. But even more, I wanted to be with Mary Anne. She knows a lot about feelings. She'd be able to explain things to me.

Suddenly I felt very homesick.

14th CHAPTER

OK, no more Miss Nice Girl. I was ready to take action, this time for real. The We ♥ Kids Club *had* to change.

I reached the end of my tether when Sunny called me on Tuesday night. She'd gone to her sitting job, the one she'd double-booked. She'd been in a great mood, knowing that I'd bailed her out.

Unfortunately, she'd forgotten to confirm with Mrs Walsh, the mother of her charge. Mrs Walsh, thinking Sunny was over-booked and that she had no sitter, had cancelled the meeting she was supposed to go to. A very important meeting, judging from how angry she was with Sunny.

This wasn't good for business. I called a special club meeting. I asked the girls to meet at Sunny's house at exactly ten o'clock on Saturday morning. That would give us plenty of time to discuss our future. I told them that the meeting would start promptly, no matter how many of us were there.

Shades of Kristy Thomas! I *never* thought I'd hear myself bossing people around like that.

It worked, though. Everyone arrived by 9:55. And everyone started talking at once.

"Mrs Walsh chewed my ear off," Sunny reported. "She told me she'd never call any of us again."

"Mr Fackler told me we ought to be more organized," Maggie said.

"He should talk!" Jill replied. "He and his wife can't decide who should make the appointments."

"Doesn't his voice sound familiar?" Sunny said. "Like Mr Ed, the talking horse?"

I wasn't going to let us get side-tracked again. "Excuse me!" I interrupted. "Let's make a list of our problems, OK? Then, when we've done that, we'll make a list of possible solutions."

My friends nodded, as if they'd just heard Abraham Lincoln speak. I took a sheet of paper from Sunny's desk and drew a line down the middle.

"OK, problems?" I asked.

Sunny: "Double-booking"

Maggie: "Who controls the record book?"

Jill: "We don't know who's doing what job."

Maggie: "Parents have to make too many calls if one of us isn't at home, or has already booked a job."

Sunny: "My mum accepted a job for me when I wasn't there, the night before a big test."

I scribbled furiously. Then I said, "Solutions?"

The room became absolutely silent.

"What about regular meeting times?" I asked.

Jill complained that that sounded too rigid. Maggie said it would be a hassle to call all our clients and tell them about the change. To that, Sunny remarked we might not *have* any more clients if Mrs Walsh told her friends what had happened.

We talked and talked. At last we settled on a plan:

1. We would have regular meeting times. Every week. (But no guilt trips about lateness.)

2. We would divide up our clients and each notify several of them that they had to call Sunny's number during meeting hours.

3. We would use the record book and check it before confirming a job.

But that was it. We decided not to appoint officers or keep a club notebook. Which was all right. Deciding on *any* rules was a big step with this group.

By the end of the meeting we were pretty pleased with ourselves. The We ♥ Kids Club would still be relaxed and fun.

Just a lot more efficient.

I was dying to tell Stephie. She'd be thrilled to hear that double-booking was a thing of the past. Besides, I wanted her to know that I still had time for her, even though things had been crazy lately.

As I walked to her house, I felt better than I had in a long time. And not only because of the W ♥ KC. It had been two weeks since my plane trip, and the atmosphere in my house was lightening. Carol had actually kept up a fair noise level the last time she'd been over.

I'd never thought I'd be happy about *that*.

Stephie answered when I knocked at her door. *"Dawn!"* she exclaimed, her face breaking into a huge grin. "What are you doing here?"

"I just dropped by to say hi and tell you some good news," I answered.

I described our meeting. Stephie's

reaction wasn't exactly what I'd expected. She shook her head and said, "I can't believe you girls are thirteen and you've only just thought of that."

Before I could reply, she ran inside, calling, "I have to show you my book!"

She came back a few moments later with a small stack of looseleaf paper, folded in half and stapled together.

The cover showed a drawing of a little girl asleep on the ground. A huge, smiling flower with arms was cradling her.

The flower had long blonde hair.

"That's me, isn't it?" I asked softly.

Stephie giggled. "It's not you, silly. It *looks* like you, and it's *named* after you. But it's just part of a *story*!"

I couldn't help laughing. Poor, sad little Stephie? She was going to be all right.

When I got back to my house, I rang Mary Anne.

"Hi!" she said. "How are you? Did you have that big meeting you were telling me about?"

"Yes," I replied. "And you won't believe what happened."

"Good news or bad?"

"Good."

"Great! Wait a minute, Dawn. Kristy's here. I want her to hear."

She called Kristy, who ran upstairs and picked up the other phone. I told them what had happened in great detail.

I was sure Kristy would disapprove. After all, we weren't adopting *all* of the BSC rules. But do you know what she said? "I think you're on the right track."

"I mean, we'll never be as organized as the BSC," I added.

"I know," Kristy replied. "And we'll never be as famous as the We Love Kids Club."

Uh-oh! I didn't want to get into *that*.

"But that's OK," Kristy went on. "Fame isn't so important." She took a deep breath. "I was actually jealous of your group for a while. Can you believe that?"

"Really?" (I was glad Kristy couldn't see the smile on my face.) "Well, to tell you the truth, all that publicity was a pain in the neck. You should be proud that the BSC is doing so well without that kind of attention."

"Thanks to your brain, Kristy," Mary Anne said.

"Yes?" Kristy replied. "Well, I suppose you've got a point. I mean, we're doing all right."

More good news. Kristy and I were friends again. I don't think she'd apologized to the BSC, but that was OK.

With Kristy, you take what you can get.

15th CHAPTER

"Hey, Dawn!" Jeff came running into my room. "What did the man say who wanted to taste some roasted goat at a restaurant?"

I looked up from my homework. "I don't know, Jeff. I've never ordered it, myself."

"It's a *joke*!" (What a surprise.) "Please pass the butt-er! *Get it?* Because a goat *butts*, and he said—"

"I get it! Now let me do my homework. Go and phone Robin Williams or something."

"That wasn't funny," Jeff said, stalking out.

It was six-thirty. Dad and Carol had gone out for an early dinner, and they probably wouldn't be back before eight-thirty or nine. So I was doomed to spend two more hours in a house with the worst joke-teller on the West coast. Very soon I would actually have to endure a meal with him.

Pure torture.

Before long I couldn't stand the hunger. I closed my books and headed for the kitchen.

That was when I heard the familiar *click* of a key in the front door, and Dad's muffled voice outside.

Salvation!

Jeff wandered into the kitchen. "What are they doing home so early?"

I heard the front door swing open. "No, of course you don't see my point," Dad was saying. "You're still wrapped up in your fantasy."

"*Fantasy?*" Carol sounded shocked. "Is it a *fantasy* to want to see a film once in a blue moon? Is it a fantasy to want to spend a little time with the person you're going to marry?"

"Uh-oh!" Jeff muttered.

"I think we'd better get out of the way," I said. "Follow me."

I ran into my bedroom, with Jeff at my heels. We shut the door softly behind us.

"Face reality, Carol." Dad's voice rang through the house. "I'm not a college student. I've got a family. You knew that when you met me."

"Well, what am *I*? We're getting married, Jack, so that makes me family, too! Is there some sort of rating system—kids first,

135

divorced wife second, new wife at the bottom of the heap?"

"Carol, you couldn't be at the bottom of any heap. You'd push yourself right to the top!"

"And what do you mean by *that*?"

Jeff and I were crouched near the door. "That sounds like a compliment to me," my brother whispered.

"It's not," I said. "Ssshh!"

"Carol, we go out once or twice a week. And you're over at the house just about every day. Soon you'll be living here. What more do you want? Restaurant-hopping every night? We're both a little too old for that."

"Speak for yourself."

"*That* wasn't a compliment," Jeff informed me.

SLAM! went the door to Dad's bedroom. The argument became muffled, but if they thought they were out of earshot, they were wrong.

I heard Dad call Carol immature. I heard her call him preoccupied. Soon they were practically screaming.

Then suddenly they stopped. Jeff's eyes widened. "Have they killed each other?"

"Sssh!"

Carol was sobbing. Dad's voice grew soft and comforting. I breathed a sigh of relief.

"Oooh, they're *making up*," Jeff said with a wicked grin.

At last I opened my bedroom door. We stepped out of our prison. (That's what it felt like.)

"Come on," I said to Jeff, "let's get something to eat."

We rummaged around in the fridge. I took out a yummy-looking salad. Jeff found cheese and bread and frozen fish sticks.

Just as we were sitting down, I heard Dad's bedroom door open.

A piece of chewed carrot got stuck in my throat. I coughed and swallowed.

Carol walked into the kitchen. Her eyes were dry, but she looked tired and glum. "Goodnight, Dawn. Goodnight, Jeff," she said.

I was glad she and Dad had made up. The argument had been scary. "See you tomorrow," I replied, trying to sound cheerful.

Carol was already halfway to the front door. "Goodbye," was all she said.

Jeff and I looked at Dad. He was leaning against the kitchen door frame, looking at the floor.

He shifted his weight and let out a sigh. Then he glanced at us. His eyes were glazed. "Kids, Carol and I have decided to stop seeing each other."

His words hung in the air for a moment.

"You mean the engagement's off?" I asked.

"No, the whole *relationship* is off."

Be careful what you wish for. It might come true. The words popped into my head, just as I'd seen them in Mal's letter. It was something Vanessa had said to Nicky.

I'd got my wish.

I felt dizzy. None of this would have happened if I hadn't been such a spoiled baby.

"I'm so sorry, Dad," I managed to say. "I didn't want this."

Dad sat down next to me. He smiled, but his eyes were still sad. "It's not your fault, Sunshine. We just weren't meant to be married, that's all."

"Oh, Dad, I know my trip to Connecticut has got something to do with it," I said. "I know what it did to Carol."

"Listen, Dawn. Carol and I had problems long ago. Your trip brought some things to a head, that's for sure. But now it's clear to me that we'd have broken up eventually anyway. You may even have done us a favour. It would have been worse to go ahead with the wedding. You know what it's like to break up *after* you're married."

"Much worse," Jeff agreed.

We ate dinner together, hardly saying a

word. Part of me felt happy. Carol was out of my life, where I'd wanted her to be for a long time. But most of me felt awfully guilty. I had no business driving Dad and Carol apart. Even if it was meant to happen, it should have happened by itself.

I think Jeff knew how I was feeling. He didn't tell one joke for the rest of the evening. Then, before he went to bed, he came into my room and said, "Don't worry, Dawn. Maybe they'll get back together."

I smiled. "Yes, maybe. Thanks."

He said goodnight and went to his room. As I got ready for bed, I thought about the future. Maybe Dad would get back together with Carol. Maybe he'd find another girlfriend he wanted to marry. Sooner or later, the situation was bound to come up again. What would I do?

Maybe I'd be in Connecticut by then. If not, I know one thing for sure. I would deal with it. Maturely. Calmly.

But before I sank into bed, I found the piece of paper on which I'd written Dad's credit card number. I ripped it into little pieces and let them drop into the waste-paper basket.

Just in case.